Tyger! Tyger!

Tyger! Tyger!
A Novel

Walter J. Roers

NORTH STAR PRESS OF ST. CLOUD, INC.
St. Cloud, Minnesota

Copyright © 2013 Walter J. Roers

All rights reserved.

ISBN: 978-0-87839-665-8

Cover art © Christopher Roers
Author photo © Karen Beltz

This is a work of fiction. Names, characters, places, and incidents are the products of the author's imagination or are used fictitiously. Any resemblance to actual events or persons, living or dead, is entirely coincidental.

First edition: September 1, 2013

Printed in the United States of America

Published by
North Star Press of St. Cloud, Inc.
P.O. Box 451
St. Cloud, MN 56302

www.northstarpress.com   North Star Press - Facebook   North Star Press - Twitter

To Myles and Alexis

The Tyger
(from *Songs of Experience*)

Tyger! Tyger! burning bright
In the forests of the night,
What immortal hand or eye
Could frame thy fearful symmetry?

. . . When the stars threw down their spears,
And watered heaven with their tears,
Did he smile his work to see?
Did he who made the Lamb make thee?

—William Blake

Prologue

I AM NOT A SCRUPULOUS READER of the daily obituaries, not yet anyway, but I have reached an age at which I give them a bit more than a casual glance. And so it was that several weeks ago a name which I hadn't heard in over fifty years caught my eye. It took a few moments before I was able to give the name some context and detail, as if I were trying to recall the plot line and characters of some long forgotten story. It would have helped had the obituary cited the nickname he was known by when he was young—Junior—but that had evidently been lost somewhere in those many intervening years. But it was as I suspected. It was Junior Kandowski.

"Kandowski, James, age 70, survived by wife, Helen . . ." the obituary began. I learned that Junior had a daughter, two sons, three grandchildren and many nieces and nephews. He had graduated from Augsburg College, served in the Army and retired after working for thirty-five years for General Mills. He was involved in volunteer work at a local community center, was an avid golfer and loved to travel. There was a picture of Junior as a young man, leaning against a basket-weave fence, arms folded, his head held at a jaunty angle, his chin thrust forward, displaying a broad smile as he squinted his eyes against the brilliant sunlight. There was no picture of him as an older man and no cause of death given. Details of the visitation and funeral service were listed and I made a note of them.

The brevity of the notice struck me as sorely inadequate and, in some deeply felt personal way, a somewhat depressing matter. As with any life, there was clearly much more to be told. I suppose it was an odd reaction on my part, as an obituary is obviously limited in its intent and scope. Yet as I sat and stared at the picture of Junior as a young man, I felt an aching sadness at such an unceremonious notice. As I read the obituary for a second time and thought back to shared moments of our youth, I found myself caught up in an inexplicable welling of emotion. I wanted something more, some description of his character, some finely crafted prose to convey to the reader a true sense of loss, because I knew the significance of his life had to have been so much larger and more profound than what was described in those few short lines of remembrance.

One

I FIRST MET JUNIOR in the early autumn of 1958. We were entering our sophomore year at South High School in Minneapolis—the old South High, a three-story red brick building of a distinctly industrial look that occupied one entire city block between Twenty-fourth and Twenty-fifth Streets on Cedar Avenue, not its present-day successor which lies a mile or so farther south. The old school drew its student body from a wide swath of the southeastern portion of the city, largely the offspring of mechanics, welders, bricklayers, factory workers, truck drivers, railroad laborers and service people.

Often members of the second or third generation to attend the school, there was without question a fierce pride in being a South High Tiger. Fathers and uncles and older brothers and cousins had been Tigers, and generations of families were known for their legendary prowess in sports. If someone had a particular surname, others knew that the individual was a member of a hockey family that had sent members on to play for the University of Minnesota and even U.S. Olympic teams. Another name represented basketball and still another represented football.

In an attempt to become part of this proud athletic tradition, I had decided to try out for the football team. I probably knew less about the game than most of those at the pre-season sessions and at five-foot-ten and one-hundred-fifty pounds after a full meal, I certainly wasn't one of the more formidable figures on the field, but I had a great deal of determination and the encouragement of my friend and fellow recruit, Tom McCarthy.

The sophomore squad conducted its drills on the practice field, an expanse of patchy, thin grass that gave way to irregularly configured areas of dirt and an unused baseball diamond in its southeastern corner. This was to the east of the formal playing field, which was flanked by wooden bleachers, a running track and a rust-colored chain-link fence. The varsity team carried out its more skilled and physically intimidating practice on the formal gridiron.

The sophomore coaches needed to sort us according to raw capabilities, so many hours of the first days of practice were spent with waves of a dozen or so hopefuls, shoulder to shoulder, running short competitive sprints, one-on-one blocking and tackling drills, and pairs of players scrambling after a "loose ball" tossed on the ground between them by one of the coaches. These drills were run to the point of collective exhaustion in the hot sun of early autumn. The white practice jerseys grew gray in the deteriorating light of the afternoon and the flesh of exposed calves, forearms, necks and faces were covered with a sticky film of dirt and sweat.

On the second afternoon of practice, the sophomore squad was the last to leave the field, straggling behind the varsity players as hundreds of cleated shoes clacked across Cedar Avenue, through the gravel parking lot and down to the basement locker room. By the time I got to my locker, some of the junior and senior players were already in the showers. As I began to struggle out of my jersey, I heard someone to my right speaking to me.

"Sorry," I said, my head still tangled in my jersey. "Could you give me a hand with this?" I leaned toward the speaker, allowing him to grab the arms and shoulders of the jersey and pull it off over my head and shoulder pads. I straightened up and saw a broad-faced boy, grinning as he handed me my jersey. He stood over six feet tall. I remembered seeing him during practice and thinking he looked big enough and talented enough to play varsity. "Thanks," I said.

"You're welcome. I'm Jim Kandowski, but everyone calls me Junior. I guess we're both trying to make the sophomore squad."

"Yeah. Good to meet you, Jim—I mean, Junior," I said as we shook hands. "I'm Will Ross."

"What position do you want to play?"

"To tell you the truth, I'll play at any spot they'll give me. What about you? Are you hoping for a particular position?"

"End," he said as he closed up his locker, ready to head to the showers. "I think I have the height and decent enough speed to be a pretty good pass receiver. That's my hope anyway." He turned toward me again and smiled. "Well, good to meet you. Good luck."

"Yeah. Thanks. Good luck to you, too."

As I continued to undress, I wondered if I might be the only try-out for the team who had no idea what position he wanted to play. Before I could pursue that troublesome line of thought into a more serious bout of worry, Tom McCarthy, towel-clad and finished with his shower, came padding down the aisle of lockers. "Ross, get your ass in gear and we can drive over to Porky's for something to eat."

"Maybe you should just go ahead, Tom. I got kind of a late start here."

Tom stared at me, arms akimbo, a feigned look of exasperation on his face. "I'll wait for you in the lot, just move your ass."

"All right, all right. I'll go as fast as I can."

Most of the sixteen showerheads were still in use when I entered the room, but two on my left, near the entry, were open. I began testing the water temperature on the one nearest the door. The room was hazy with steam and the shouts and whoops of the players, including a few varsity members, ricocheted off the tiled walls and filled the space with ceaseless noise. When I had the temperature calibrated to a tolerable level of heat, I stepped under the showerhead and began to lather my scalp, my back to the eight showers on the opposite wall. It was relaxing, even in that steamy, unsettled environment, but I needed to hurry and quickly rinsed my scalp and turned my back to the water. I glanced at the other side of the room. It was a second or two before I realized what was taking place just a few feet away. I was shocked and revolted by what I saw.

One of the varsity players, a stout, curly-haired boy, was turned toward the player next to him. At first I thought the curly-haired boy was wincing in reaction to the heat of the shower, but I quickly realized that his face was contorted in a grimace of hatred and anger. And in the next instant I saw that he was urinating on the leg of the black player showering next to him. The black player was clearly unaware of what was happening. I turned back and faced the showerhead, closed my eyes and let the water rain down on my face and neck. I finished up as quickly as possible and without looking back at anyone in the room, I exited and headed back to get dressed and leave.

Junior was at his locker, halfway dressed and doing some rearrangement of his gear in the tiny storage space. "Did you see what happened in the shower?" I said, still shocked by what I'd seen and unable to banish the image from my mind.

"What?" Junior asked, evidently distracted by the disorder in his locker.

I leaned toward him, kept my voice low and repeated, "Did you see what happened in the shower?"

"No. What happened?"

"One of the white varsity players was peeing on one of the colored guys. I'm not sure, but I think the colored guy was Joe Washington, the best running back on the team. I couldn't believe it. This guy was pissing all over his leg."

Junior's face grew sober, almost grave. "You sure?"

"Yeah, I was looking right at them."

"What did you do?"

"Nothing. I mean, what could I do? I finished my shower as fast as I could and I got the hell out of there."

"Yeah," Junior said. He didn't say anything more, but stood and stared into his locker. I waited, but he just continued to stare into his locker and say nothing.

"God, I couldn't believe it. I mean, it was . . . it was really ugly."

"Yeah," Junior repeated at last, then slammed his locker door shut and finished dressing without saying anything further. I could sense his anger, but I had no idea if it was because of what had happened, if it was directed at me because I had done nothing about it, or perhaps both. His brooding silence grew to what seemed a tangible barrier between us and I said nothing more to him as I dressed.

When I got out to the parking lot, Tom was leaning back against his black, two-door 1950 Ford, his hands shoved deep into the pockets of his khaki pants, his head tilted back, his eyes closed.

"About time," he shouted without opening his eyes.

"Sorry, Tom," I said hurriedly as we scrambled into the car.

"Hey, there's a pack of Luckies in the glove compartment. Go ahead and have one, if you want," he said.

"How about if we get at least a block from the school before we light up?"

"Okay, Will the Worrier, but shake one out of the pack for me."

As we headed south along Cedar Avenue, I told him about what I had seen in the shower. Tom listened as he lit a cigarette and jammed the lighter back into the dash.

"Yeah? Who was the white guy?"

"I don't know. Kind of fat, real curly hair. I'm not sure who he is."

Tom squinted as he held the cigarette in his mouth and the smoke curled back against his face. "Yeah, well you know what they say: better to be pissed off than pissed on." He stomped down on the gas and raced through an amber light as the tires shrieked against the pavement.

I was sorry immediately that I'd said anything about the incident to Tom. His reaction was exactly what I could have expected—dismissive and without empathy. I had known him since we were kids in Holy Rosary Catholic grade school. He was a fiercely loyal friend and generous with whatever he possessed, but there was a toughness about him that hardened his reaction to anyone or anything that existed beyond his circle of friends and the circumscribed world he had defined for himself.

Two

On Twenty-fourth Street, on the corner directly across Cedar Avenue from South High, was Lida's Café. A squat, cream-colored stucco building, its daytime patrons were almost exclusively students from the high school who wished to smoke without fear of sanctions of any kind. Entering Lida's, the most striking features were the ever-present blue haze of cigarette smoke and the booming Wurlitzer jukebox that occupied the center of the café floor. High-backed wooden booths ran along three of the walls and a counter with a half-dozen stools completed the perimeter of the one-room eatery. At times I wondered, how ever fleetingly, how Lida was able to make a living from her tiny café. She hurried back and forth in her shop, a gray-haired woman who endured her teenage patrons with cryptic silence, selling only an occasional sandwich or burger to accompany the endless rounds of Coke and Pepsi.

Though not aware of whatever technical or legal protections might really exist, or how long they might stay in place, I was one of many students who at times rushed to Lida's over the lunch hour to smoke with impunity. Like so many others, I believed her café enjoyed some shielded status from school authorities that we might as well enjoy, even if it wasn't fully understood.

On a Wednesday in mid-September, I hurried to Lida's after bolting down my lunch. I was craving a cigarette. I also hoped to see Tom there and find out what plans he had for the weekend. I was nearly to the corner when I overtook Gloria Jensen, the most distracting girl in biology and, in my opinion, the most attractive girl in the sophomore class. In my hurry to get to Lida's, it wasn't until I was alongside her that I became aware that it was Gloria. As I began to pass her on the street side, she turned and spoke, breaking through my thoughts.

"Hi, Will. Are you headed home for lunch?"

"Oh, Gloria. I didn't see you. I mean, I didn't know it was you," I said, fumbling. I seemed to fumble often around Gloria. Something about her smile and directness unnerved me and made me inordinately self-conscious. "Uh, no, I'm headed over to Lida's. How about you, are you going to Lida's?"

Gloria smiled generously, her shoulder-length auburn hair shiny in the sun. Her brown eyes narrowed and almost disappeared as she smiled. "No. I go home for lunch, it's just a few blocks."

"Oh, sure," I said. I didn't know Gloria well, but I knew she didn't smoke and guessed that she had never set foot inside Lida's—and probably never would, unless it provided the only escape from an attack dog or some other untold danger. "I mean, I should have known that," I said, trying to recover. "I mean, I don't go there very often either—not that you'd go there at all, but I don't go there much." I stopped talking. Silence seemed less painful than anything else I might say.

"Why don't you walk me across Cedar and I'll see you in biology this afternoon," she said, her smile still full and warm.

We crossed the avenue and said goodbye. I stopped at the door to Lida's and watched her as she continued on along Twenty-fourth Street. I recalled our brief conversation in detail, trying to make my part sound less spectacularly foolish. I went over it several times, but I couldn't really make it come out any better. Then, just as I was about to turn my gaze away from her and enter Lida's, I realized something else about Gloria that I found appealing. She had great posture. I turned to look at her again as she walked along, her back straight, her head held high. "Damn," I said to no one.

Lida's was full and the haze of cigarette smoke stung my eyes as I entered. "Little Darlin'" was playing on the jukebox, the Diamonds warning about the mistake of trying to love two. I scanned the booths and those gathered near the counter, but couldn't find Tom among the crowd. I fished a lone cigarette and matches out of my breast pocket and lit up, nodding to a couple of people I knew only slightly. I moved slowly through the crowd, checking each booth individually. The jukebox had moved on to "Get A Job" by the Silhouettes when I heard a burst of scuffling and scraping sounds from one of the back booths. It was Tom, on his feet, fists clenched at his sides. His head was thrust forward, the muscles in his thick neck strained as he challenged a larger boy who faced him.

"Go ahead, asshole," Tom growled. "I'll let you have the first punch."

The larger boy backed up slightly, while verbally giving no ground. "Not here, Jack," he said evenly. "We'll settle this another time." He was half a head taller than Tom, his face all hard edges and angles, except for an improbably small and rounded nose. The boy's face was flushed and contrasted sharply with blond hair that was so pale as to appear nearly white.

"No, right now," Tom said and leaned in closer, his chin thrust forward. Lida pushed her way through the crowd as it tightened around the two. "Take it outside," she shouted several times as she worked her way through the throng of gawking students. "Take it outside," she repeated. "None of that crap in here. Take it outside."

The larger boy turned to leave, followed by two other boys and a girl. Before he reached the door he called out over his shoulder, "We'll settle this yet, you little prick."

Tom began to move forward, blocked by Lida's upraised hand. "No!" she shouted.

Tom stopped, but hollered back, "Count on it."

As the crowd loosened up, I heard Lida tell Tom that he would need to leave, too. He nodded and raised one hand, palm forward, in a sign of assent, then picked his pack of cigarettes from the table top of the booth. I called out to him as he headed toward the door.

"Will, I didn't see you. Come on with me," he said.

I fell in step beside him. "What the hell was that all about?"

"I guess he doesn't believe in freedom of speech. He didn't like me talking to his girlfriend."

"You better lighten up, Tom. He's a pretty big guy. Do you know him, or anything about him?"

Tom looked straight ahead as we left the café, his face taut with anger, his eyes narrowed. "All I know is that he's some senior punk who thinks he's a badass." He spat the words out with contempt.

"I'm telling you Tom, one of these days you're going to tangle with the wrong guy."

"Not him—he's a front. If he was bad he would have swung on me in there." The tightness left his face and he turned toward me and smiled. "You're the one who needs to lighten up. You're wound too tight." he said, and clapped me on the back. "You're worrying again, Will. That's no way to live."

As we crossed Cedar Avenue and headed back to the school, I saw the white-haired boy and three other boys standing about halfway up the block. White Hair pointed in our direction and the three others nodded. It appeared Tom either didn't notice them or didn't care about their attention, I couldn't tell which.

"Tom, up the block," I said and nodded in the direction of White Hair.

"I see them. Don't sweat it. They're a bunch of pussies."

Three

THE BEST PART OF MY DAY was Miss Frank's biology class, because it was the one hour of the day I could be certain I would at least see Gloria, even if there was no opportunity to talk with her. No doubt many of my furtive glances were noted both by Miss Frank and Gloria, but the power of her presence was so great a force for me that I found watching her was no longer an act of volition, but as involuntary and essential as breathing. The way her calf tapered at the ankle, the pink softness that sometimes rose in her cheeks, the way she tucked her hair behind her ears as she bent over her textbook all captured my attention and produced a sort of exhilaration I had never experienced before.

There was, of course, a price to be paid for my inattention. On several occasions Miss Frank's questions caught me in mid-reverie, completely unaware of the topic under discussion or the specific item of interest at the moment. "Will, what system do spiracles open into on a grasshopper?" or "Will, can you please describe the next phase of the oxygen cycle?" would find me bewildered and embarrassed, asking if the question might be repeated. These little episodes became increasingly amusing to the other members of the class and more than once I noticed Gloria blush, her neck and cheeks pink when Miss Frank exposed my non-scientific preoccupation.

My problem had become so obvious that I began to wonder if Miss Frank might have me transferred to another hour or removed from class entirely, and still I couldn't help myself. And then the most astounding thing happened. Miss Frank divided the entire class into groups of two and three students to work on a collaborative paper and frog dissection project, and I was assigned to work with Gloria. Our team was just the two of us. Almost as quickly as the thrill of the assignment rose in me, I began to theorize why Miss Frank had paired the two of us. Perhaps she thought if we worked closely together I would come to see Gloria in what she considered a more realistic and less flattering light, allowing me to regain my composure and yet unproven powers of concentration. Maybe, knowing that Gloria was a bright and conscientious student, she thought Gloria would succeed in getting me to shoulder my share of the work and focus on the project. Or, in my most sentimental moments, I wondered if possibly Miss Frank, recalling some lost romantic opportunity from her youth, wanted us to share some part of our lives, if only the single hour that she could give us. I quickly dismissed this sentimental option when I saw the stern look on Miss Frank's face as she watched the two of us on the first day of the project.

Whatever motive may have moved Miss Frank to assign Gloria and me to partner on the project, I benefited in several ways. Gloria was, as expected, dedicated to completing the project on time and doing an excellent job, so she kept us—or rather, me—on task. That was, without question, in my best interest and undoubtedly raised the quality of the work to a level I could not have achieved alone or likely with any other partner. At the same time, there were more personal moments when she and I could take a break from the project and, in little bits and pieces of conversation, learn about each other, slowly filling in the spaces that completed, or nearly completed, our individual histories.

I learned that she was an avid reader of novels, belonged to the school French Club, was not a fan of any particular sport and hoped to soon be working part-time at a White Castle hamburger shop. Except for my hope of securing a part-time job as soon as I turned sixteen, we didn't seem to match up well initially, as my efforts at reading were essentially limited to what was required for my classes, and most of my free time, at least in the fall, was consumed by football. It was clear that I needed desperately to establish areas of mutual interest.

"So, you really like French?" I said.

"I do. I hope to go to France some day. Wouldn't you love to see Paris?"

"I would. I definitely would. I think of all the cities in Europe, that's the one I'd most like to see."

Gloria turned her head to look at me. She brushed some hair back behind her ear and furrowed her brow, as if to question my sincerity.

"I really mean it. I'd love to go to the top of that tower and look out over the city."

"The Eiffel Tower."

"Yes, the Eiffel Tower. That would be great, don't you think?"

"Yes," she said dreamily.

"I bet you can spit a mile from the top of that thing."

After a moment, Gloria laughed and slapped my shoulder. This bit of playfulness did not escape the attention of Miss Frank.

"Will and Gloria, have you already completed today's section of the assignment?"

"No, Miss Frank," we said in unison and bent back over our papers.

I learned other things about Gloria as the days passed. The Platters and The Four Lads were her favorite singing groups. She loved any movie with Montgomery Clift and she had a cat named Josephine. I learned that she was an only child, born just a few months after her father left for Germany and the war. He had never returned to Gloria and her mother, killed by a Nazi sniper in the waning days of the war, just as the German army collapsed in defeat and Russian troops approached Berlin. Her widowed mother had remained single for eight years after her father died, but eventually married a butcher who worked in a market near their home. The butcher, Martin Scully, was five years her mother's junior. Gloria was happy to never have taken his name and would never willingly call him her father. She was Carl Jensen's daughter. She would always be Carl Jensen's daughter. The personal revelations abruptly ended there, as though she had, in an unguarded moment, crossed some line that was a barrier to everyone outside her home, as if she had somehow betrayed a deeply held trust. I tried on several occasions to renew our more personal exchanges, but her interest in discussing anything outside our science project vanished and her manner grew more somber. It was no use, but I wanted so much to make her laugh again and feel the lingering, phantom touch of her hand on my shoulder as I headed home after school.

Four

Tom and Junior and I all made the sophomore football squad. Junior, as he had hoped, was given the position of offensive end. Tom and I, to my amazement, were both selected as linesmen—left and right guards, respectively. The more I learned about the game, the more I was mystified as to why the coaches had picked either of us to play on the line rather than in the backfield. Neither Tom nor I possessed the necessary size desirable for the blocking and tackling duties of guards, but we both labored at the positions and possessed an essential strength and quickness. In any event, the two of us played both offensively and defensively and the team won its first two games with very little difficulty.

Although not as frequent or intense as the pre-season training, practices continued during the week in preparation for games on Friday or Saturday afternoons. It was during these practices I first learned that Tom and I had apparently become linked in the mind of the head coach, not only because we were friends who both played at the guard position, but because of Tom's growing reputation as a street fighter. "Looks like we need a couple of tough guys," the coach would shout. "Put in McCarthy and Ross and have them bring their clubs and chains." The assistant coaches would laugh as the head coach grinned at his own little joke. "Give McCarthy and Ross some brass knuckles and they'll beat anyone across the line." I think Tom found it all amusing, maybe even flattering. I was a little surprised that Tom's reputation had gained such prominence beyond his fellow students, but most puzzling to me was that the coaches seemed to admire what I had thought they would most discourage—Tom's undisciplined emotions and violent outbursts.

It was during one of these practices that two players involved in a blocking and tackling exercise had lost control and nearly come to blows after one had thrown dirt in the other's face. As the story spread among the other team members, the details of what had happened and the identity of the victim and the aggressor changed and shifted. In one version, Leo Stevens, a white player, was the victim of Sonny Holmes, a black player. I really couldn't sort out what was fact and what was rumor, but I thought it odd that Sonny and Leo had even been paired off, as Leo easily outweighed the diminutive Sonny by forty pounds. In any event, no matter what the facts might have been, it became clear that Leo and Sonny were going to settle things after practice. Other players were being asked to stay for the fight, not because of the spectacle itself, but to be there in case the conflict grew larger.

The varsity and junior squads combined totaled fewer than a dozen black players, but not one had left the school grounds when I exited the locker room and walked out the door that led to the small parking lot on the southern end of the building. The black players stood huddled together on one side of the walk, while at least half again as many white players stood on the other side, less than twenty feet away. My first thought was to simply head home and ignore whatever was about to happen, but I sensed that my choice would not be so simple. "Stick around," someone from the crowd of white players said to me, but I kept walking. Someone grabbed my elbow. I turned and saw it was Tom.

"Hang on, Will. Let's see where this goes," he said.

"Damn it, Tom, this is stupid. Let's just leave."

"Just hang on a minute."

I stood and faced Tom, both angry at the stupidity of what might happen and frightened at the prospect of how bloody things might really become. And yet, the choices no longer seemed clear or simple. What had begun as a brief flash of anger between two teammates had now been redefined into a much larger issue. Suddenly and undeniably, this was about friendship and loyalty and divisions that ran deeper than any of us would readily admit. I glanced at the black players—our teammates and classmates who, like the white players, were now bonded by race alone. I looked beyond them, across Eighteenth Avenue, at the gray stone exterior of

Holy Rosary grade school and the nearby church, where Tom and I had been students and altar boys together. At once I thought about how much simpler life had been just a few years earlier and how much I wished at this moment that someone would find a way to stop whatever was about to unfold.

Leo Stevens stood near the front of the white crowd, but Sonny had not yet left the locker room. As the minutes passed, both groups fell into a tense silence, the white and black players not looking across the walk at each other and no longer even talking among themselves. "God, Tom," I whispered. "This is ridiculous. Let's get the hell out of here." Tom ignored me and stared silently at the door to the school as it slowly began to open.

Sonny Holmes exited. He looked frightened and tentatively stepped through the door and onto the walk. Everyone on both sides of the path watched Sonny as he approached the corridor of players. Leo Stevens took two steps forward and separated himself from the phalanx of white players. Before the door closed behind Sonny, a second player emerged. Sonny slowed his walk as Junior Kandowski caught up with him. Junior spoke briefly to Sonny and then quickly scanned the groups on either side of the walk.

"Ross," he called out to me. "Will Ross, do you need a ride anywhere? I'm giving Sonny a ride home and could drop you somewhere too, if you need a ride."

I was so stunned by what Junior was doing and that he had singled me out of the crowd that for an instant I didn't respond.

"Will, need a ride?" he called again.

"No," I finally managed to get out. "Thanks anyway, Junior, but I'm headed home and it's just a couple of blocks." And in those few words I felt a vague sense of pride in having helped Junior in what he was doing, no matter how slight my contribution.

"All right, see you tomorrow," he called back and then turned his attention to Leo. "Excuse me, Leo, Sonny and I are in kind of a hurry," he said, as he and Sonny continued on down the walk.

I watched Leo as Junior and Sonny headed toward the parking lot. He looked anxious and uncomprehending and possibly a bit relieved. He continued to stare at them wordlessly until they got into Junior's car and the doors chunked shut in rapid succession. The protesting engine started on the second attempt. For a few moments there was only the sound of the car's engine and the crunch of its tires on the gravel as it left the lot.

"I guess there's nothing happening here, man," one of the black players said to no one in particular. "See you tomorrow, Ben," he called out to one of the white players.

"Yeah, see you tomorrow," the white player called back. And it was done, at least for the moment. The two crowds broke into groups of two and three people and drifted off along the slate-colored city streets in the chill of the early autumn afternoon.

Five

Porky's drive-in was located on the eastern end of Lake Street, a heavily trafficked commercial boulevard running from the Mississippi river on the east to Lake Calhoun on the west, spanning the width of the city. Porky's was one of the more popular stopping points for the stream of adolescent-laden cars that wandered back and forth on weekend nights in search of excitement in whatever form it might appear.

Tom and I had been cruising Lake Street for nearly an hour one Saturday night and by the time we pulled into Porky's, it was nearly nine o'clock. It was warm for late September and there were several convertibles, tops down, among the cars crowding the perimeter of the lot. Neither of us saw any familiar cars or faces as we searched for a parking space. On a second pass around the horseshoe-shaped circuit, we backed into an open space and ordered two Twinburgers, Porky's greasiest offering, fries and Cokes and settled back in our seats as the smoke from our cigarettes wafted out the windows into the clear night air.

"I think I'm about ready to call it a night, Tom."

Tom was watching a pea-green, customized 1949 Mercury that had just entered the lot and was slowly parading in front of the parked cars and the tray toting carhops who scurried about the lot.

"That's Pipsqueak's car," Tom said.

"Who the hell is Pipsqueak?"

"Pipsqueak Preston. He goes to Roosevelt," he said, referring to our school's chief rival. "He knows just about everyone in South Minneapolis. If anyone knows about any action tonight, it's Pipsqueak," he said hurriedly. "Hey, Pipsqueak, talk to me," Tom shouted at the Mercury. The driver waved in response.

Before our order had arrived, a diminutive figure, gnome-like and wearing an oversized, red crewneck sweater, appeared at Tom's window. Pipsqueak's smile was constant as he spoke with Tom.

"Hey, Tom, what's going on?"

"That's what I was going to ask you. Where's the action tonight?"

"Haven't heard too much. Hey, who's your friend?"

"This is Will. He wants to know what's going on, too."

"Hi, Will," Pipsqueak said as he nodded in my direction.

"Hi ya," I said, omitting what seemed to me to be an especially insulting nickname.

"There's a party at Jackie Delaney's house, about a block east of Duffy's bar on Twenty-sixth. Do you know Jackie? She's a junior at South."

"I think so," Tom said.

"It doesn't matter, you guys can get in. If you and Will need some beer, I can get it for you."

"No thanks, Pipsqueak. I doubt we can afford it," Tom said.

Pipsqueak gave no indication of being insulted, his ingratiating smile unrelenting. "No, man, I sell it to you same as what I pay for it."

"It's okay, we're good. You better get back to your car now. The off-duty is heading your way."

Pipsqueak glanced over his shoulder to see an off-duty cop advancing in his direction. He tapped twice on Tom's door. "So long, man. Take it easy," he said and then turned toward the cop. "Headed back to my car, Officer," he said and raised both hands above his head, palms exposed.

I turned to Tom. "I'd just as soon pass on the party, Tom—and any beer, too."

"Hey, your old man's working tonight, right? So what's the problem?"

"I just . . . I don't know. I guess I don't feel like partying, that's all."

Tom gave me a long stare, his frustration palpable. "We'll just check it out. We won't stay more than an hour."

* * * * *

Twenty minutes later we parked a half-block from Jackie Delaney's house. I could hear the rhythmic thump of music and the drone of voices punctuated by laughter as we approached. A dozen or so people milled about the tiny front yard bordered by a gated, chain-link fence. Each person held a bottle of beer or a drink. Most were talking loudly and some showed signs of imbalance as they shuffled in or out of the shotgun-style house, letting the screen door bang shut each time. Someone in the yard said hello to Tom and me as we neared the house, his voice unfamiliar and his features indistinct in the darkness.

The body heat and din inside the house could both be felt physically upon entry. The beat of the music resonated in my chest. Somewhere, a stereo turned to its maximum volume blared above the voices. The Coasters were singing "Yakety Yak," but their tale of teenage angst appeared lost on the throng and of no real interest to anyone.

Tom went to the kitchen to search for beer while I worked my way through the crowd in the living room. A couple in an overstuffed chair sat in a far corner, kissing passionately, seemingly unaware of the people surrounding them. A couch along an outside wall was filled with drinking, smoking revelers, one no longer conscious as his cigarette burned dangerously close to his fingers.

I noticed a tall girl whose hair had the sheen and blackness of a crow's wing. She pushed her way through the partiers and cleaned up spills, cleared away ashtrays and plucked the burning cigarette from the hand of the boy who had passed out on the couch. I assumed the black-haired girl was Jackie Delaney, trying to protect her parent's home against damage, doing her best to bring some control to a gathering that was quickly becoming chaotic. At a glance I could see panic rising in her eyes as she realized that her efforts were being overwhelmed.

"Hey, Jack," came a voice from behind me. There was something sinister and threatening in the tone and I didn't turn immediately. "I'm talking to you, Jack. Aren't you the buddy of Mr. Hard-ass?"

I turned to face the voice. "Are you talking to me?" I said, and immediately recognized the tall boy with hair that appeared even whiter now than it had when I first saw him at Lida's. "The name's Will."

"No shit. That's real interesting, Jack. Seems to me I saw you at Lida's. Is your hard-ass friend with you?"

A shorter, more muscular boy standing next to him spoke. "Lida ain't here. Nick, maybe he don't go nowhere unless he's got some woman to protect him." He said it with a sneer and then snickered at his own fine humor.

"Is that right, Jack? Does your buddy hide behind skirts?" He emphasized his question with a poke to my shoulder with his beer-free hand.

Tom had just stepped into the room and stood behind my two inquisitors. "You could ask him yourself. He's standing right behind you," I said.

Nick and his friend executed a fast pivot and faced Tom. "Well, if it isn't Mr. Hard-ass. Wanna step outside now, tough guy?"

Tom smiled. "I do," he said calmly. "You can bring your little girlfriend, too."

The muscular boy looked enraged, but something about Tom's unshaken demeanor seemed to jolt Nick. He was unable to mask a look of uncertainty, perhaps even fear. He turned to his friend. "You come with me, Artie, but I'll handle this myself."

The two headed out the front door with Tom close behind. As he passed me, Tom tapped me on the chest. "Come on, back me up on this."

My heart raced and I could feel my hands begin to shake. "Aw, shit, Tom."

"C'mon, back me up."

As we stepped outside, Nick bent down toward the sidewalk, swung his right hand in a quick looping motion and broke the bottom off his bottle of beer. The explosive sound of the foaming beer and shattered glass silenced everyone in the front yard, and then Nick spun around, the jagged remains of the bottle now held out in front of him toward Tom. "Come on, asshole," he shouted. His voice cracked with excitement or fear and caused the word "asshole" to shriek out as some errant high note that suspended itself in the air and lingered above the silent yard.

Tom feinted to his left and simultaneously kicked at Nick's right hand, sending the remains of the bottle clattering to the walk. And then they were at each other, fists and feet colliding with bone and flesh and muscle. It was too dark to see everything that was happening, but from the sound I knew they were fighting furiously, unleashing every bit of strength and hatred in the most destructive assaults they could muster. Between the torrents of blows could be heard snatches of guttural sounds and increasingly labored breathing.

My mind raced as the fight continued. I watched Artie and hoped that he would continue to stand aside. The sounds of the fight slowed momentarily, both combatants now breathless from the exertion. Someone had fallen or been knocked to the ground and then they were both on the ground and I could hear fists striking again in rapid combinations of two and three blows. In the midst of all this, among the onlookers and Artie and the music that blared from the house and the odor of fallen leaves and beer and damp grass, one unexpected thought eclipsed everything around me. As the two of them used their final measure of strength and will in an attempt to prevail, I was struck by the incredible pointlessness of the struggle. And that single thought became more salient and real than anything in the enveloping darkness.

I could hear Tom's voice, raspy and low, and I could see that he was on top of Nick now, his knee in Nick's back as he held his right arm twisted up behind him. With his other hand, Tom held Nick's face back away from the sidewalk with a fistful of white hair. I could see a thick, dark stream running down beneath Nick's nose onto his mouth and chin. "Enough, or do you want to eat some cement?"

Nick spat, but said nothing. He was in a helpless position and appeared drained of all energy and ability to resist, yet was not willing to humiliate himself—not just yet.

"You hear me?" Tom shouted and pulled his head back farther.

Nick finally exhaled just one word, "Enough." Tom released him and got to his feet.

Six

THE SOPHOMORE FOOTBALL SQUAD'S season ended with just two losses and the second best record in the city. The colors of autumn faded to pewter-gray skies and barren tress that awaited the first snows of the Minnesota winter. I looked forward to the week-long Christmas break with both anticipation and misgivings. My older sister and only sibling, Denise, would be home on break from college in St. Cloud, and I was anxious to see her again. There would be a visit to our cousins in St. Paul, midnight Mass at Holy Rosary on Christmas Eve and turkey dinner at home on Christmas Day. On the other hand, I probably would not see Gloria for the entire week, lacking both a car and freedom from family obligations. Our friendship had reached some frustrating plateau, neither lessening nor intensifying—except in my thoughts and desires.

More than the holiday break, I was looking forward to January, the new year and my sixteenth birthday. At sixteen I would be able to hold a job and get my driver's license, and possibly a car of my own. I could also use my earnings to dress in style: button-down shirts by Gant, wing-tip shoes, khaki pants and a leather sleeved "hero jacket." All this, I hoped, might be obtainable with little or no need to seek help from my parents. And all this, I understood without consciously admitting it to myself, was related to Gloria.

While I was preoccupied with these thoughts, I knew my materialistic goals would be under pressure for some trimming. When I began earning money, I had no doubt that my parents would insist I set a portion of it aside for education after high school, just as they had with Denise. Concerns about saving for college seemed so distant, abstract and unrealistic to me that I was able to swat such ideas away from my daydreams of cars and clothing and Gloria with relative ease. After all, I reasoned in moments of what I considered cold and geometric logic, Denise had always been a much better student, consistently receiving As in nearly all classes and winning a partial scholarship to teacher's college. The Army and learning a trade seemed a more reasonable post-high school path for me. This line of thought seemed ultimately sensible to me, but would probably not, I knew, be persuasive to my parents.

Our father, with no education beyond high school and battered by the Great Depression of the 1930s, was passionate to the point of irrational fervor about education and saving and preparing oneself for a life's career. Denise and I had become familiar at an early age with stories of how our parents had lost their first home during the Depression, how there had been food riots in Minneapolis, how people sold apples on street corners and how folks had wondered aloud why a man in their neighborhood had killed himself when he was fortunate enough to own a new pair of shoes. But, as may always be the case, it was difficult for us to believe in the youth of our father, so the stories lacked a certain reality and lost much of whatever sting they may have possessed in the many years of retelling.

For the past twenty years he had worked as a brakeman on the Northern Pacific railroad, and gave whatever financial support he could to Denise's education. He was pleased she was able to contribute so much through her own savings and academic accomplishments. Our mother worked part-time as a sales clerk at a dress shop on Lake Street. With two incomes, they were able to secure a modest three-bedroom rambler, a family car which was usually no more than three or four years old at the time of purchase and sometimes provide for a brief family vacation in summer, usually at a rented lake cabin somewhere in northern Minnesota. But it was understood that Denise and I were largely responsible for our lives beyond high school, and cars or expensive clothing were luxuries in adolescence we would need to secure on our own. "You're lucky to have food on the table each night," our father would intone. "When your mother and I were young you could buy a spaghetti dinner for two people for a dime—and nobody had a lousy dime. You kids today have no idea how lucky you are."

None of my father's admonitions could discourage me. None of his cautionary tales could dissuade me. My priorities were unshakable. And then one night at dinner, just three nights before Christmas, I realized that if no one else could understand the passion and urgency of my dreams, Denise could.

The four of us were nearly done with dinner and our parents' conversation had drifted into an assessment of the latest popular music—base and unskilled and degenerate. I stared distractedly out our front window, as I had heard this discussion before. In the cone of amber light beneath the corner streetlamp, I could see a new snow falling. The flakes were large and drifted slowly into the light, and then tumbled like wounded moths to the ground.

"I've met a really wonderful guy at school." Denise said as a sort of general announcement.

My father stared at her, his knife and fork suspended, motionless, above his plate. He said nothing, and then gazed at our mother in what was an apparent cue for her to speak. He tried to keep his emotions hidden, as was so often the case.

"Do we know him, honey?" Mom asked.

Denise looked at all of us and smiled, clearly excited to tell us her news. "No, he's not from around here. He's from Duluth and going into teaching, too. We had two classes together this quarter. I had kind of hoped he could meet all of you on Christmas break, but he had to spend his time at home."

I stopped my snowgazing and turned my attention to Denise. "What's his name, Dee?" I asked.

"Don Christianson, and he's a wonderful guy," she repeated. "He's done so many things and has seen so much of the world."

Our father remained speechless, his knife and fork still suspended above his plate. Mom appeared somewhat jarred by the worldly résumé of Denise's friend and took time to pat her hair and brush imaginary crumbs from her lap before she spoke again. "What do you mean about him seeing so much of the world?" she asked at last.

"He was in the Navy after high school and traveled all around the Pacific. He saw the most fascinating things," Denise answered.

Dad's silverware clattered noisily against his plate as his silence gave way to somewhat hostile agitation. "Just how old is this man? I mean, you're in college, Denise, but you're still just eighteen years old."

"Nineteen," Mom said reflexively.

"Oh, hell. All right, she's nineteen, but I want to know about this—this sailor. How old is this guy?"

Denise's composure was not ruffled in the least. I knew she would be able to calm Dad. She had had that ability from the time she was a little girl. "Dad," she said slowly, her dimpled smile even broader, and with that single word she recognized his motivation to protect her and at the same time assured him that there was no need for alarm. "He's twenty-two years old. You'd like him, I'm sure of it. He treats me with great respect. And it's more than that, really. It's like we've always known each other somehow. I know that's impossible and sounds ridiculous, but I've never been more happy and comfortable with someone."

"Comfortable," Dad snorted, clearly still distressed.

"Dad," Denise said again and reached across the table to pat his hand. "I know you'll like him. You'll be happy to know that he's Catholic—and a Democrat."

"Mmmmm," was our father's only immediate response, but the news of his political allegiance, even more perhaps than his religious affiliation, brought a degree of calm to Dad's facial expression and the building tension in his hands and shoulders instantly vanished. "Well, we'll see. You bring him around some time."

* * * * *

A LITTLE BEFORE TEN O'CLOCK that night I tapped on Denise's bedroom door.

"Yes."

"It's me. Could I talk with you for a few minutes?"

"Sure, come on in, Will."

As I entered the room, she set aside a book she was reading. "Dostoyevsky," she said. "I could use a break." She added the book to a small stack on the nightstand. "I thought I'd get a head start. It's required in a literature course next quarter." She was under her down comforter, flannel-clad in red plaid pajamas. She drew her knees up toward her chin and patted a spot on the bed where I was to sit. "What's up, little brother?"

"You look real cute in those flannel pajamas,"

"Yeah, yeah, they're warm. Just tell me what you want, smart guy."

I dropped onto the designated spot on the bed. "I guess I don't know exactly where to begin with this. When you were talking about your friend, Don, it made me think about a girl I've met at school."

"Ah, is little brother in love?"

"Dee, come on."

"Okay, sorry. No more kidding. What did you want to tell me?"

"I really do like this girl, and I think she likes me, but I don't see her at all outside class, which is a problem, of course. We worked on a biology project together and everything was great until she started to talk about her family one day. All of a sudden she clammed up on me. It was like she had revealed some secret and was going to be executed for it. Ever since then she's friendly and all, but nothing is going anywhere. Do you know what I mean?"

"I think so. What did she tell you?"

"Nothing, really, just that her dad was killed in the war and that her mom waited something like eight years before she remarried. I think she isn't too crazy about her stepfather, but she really didn't say too much."

"Go on."

I talked with Dee for an hour or so, doing my best to explain how I felt about Gloria and how I felt so powerless to date her when I had no car and no money and really nothing to offer. She listened patiently, and let me ramble on without interruption. Her advice was simple and direct.

"You don't need a car or money to get to know her—or for her to get to know you. Besides, you must have friends for double dating, if you want to ask her out. Or you could always just ask her to go for a walk. Something may be bothering her, so just be her friend. Listen to her. Let her get to know you and trust you—a lot of that can be done just with phone calls. Most of all, give her time, little brother."

Later, as I lay in my bed, I looked out at the snow that continued to fall, transforming cars and trees and rooftops into a world of white on white. I watched and thought of Gloria, wondering if she was asleep at that moment, hoping that her world was as hushed and peaceful and beautiful as the deepening white expanse outside my window.

Seven

CHRISTMAS BREAK CAME AND WENT, with Dee returning to classes at St. Cloud just before my sixteenth birthday. She had returned to school as the owner of a new transistor radio, a makeup kit and a bottle of Chanel No. 5 perfume. My gifts, which covered both Christmas and my birthday, consisted entirely of clothing: four pair of socks, two crewneck sweaters, blue jeans and a new pair of gloves, none of which were the more prized items of fashion for which I had hoped. Dee and I, with Dee's money, had given our parents a new set of water glasses, a Nat King Cole album for Mom and a carton of Camels for Dad.

A group from school had organized a tobogganing party on the last Friday night before we were to return to classes. I joined Tom and a group of nine other sophomore boys and girls in a caravan of three cars to Theodore Wirth Park near downtown. We tobogganed the tree-lined slopes until our hands and feet were damp and painful from the cold, a joyful exercise of trudging breathlessly uphill, feet splayed, hauling the toboggan behind us, and then racing again to the bottom to repeat the process. Near the end of the evening, after two consecutive runs in which I managed to sustain sharp blows to my right knee, I begged off the final few rides. I stood alone and watched the others on the last runs of the night, the toboggans careening down the blue, moonlit paths of snow twisting between the black pines and leafless oaks and maples, shouts and screams fading on the wind as my classmates raced down the slope. I looked at the canopy of crystalline stars and puffed clouds of my breath skyward, wishing Gloria had been among the group.

I had taken Dee's advice and called Gloria twice while on break. On both occasions her stepfather answered the phone. Both times he told me that Gloria wasn't available. He didn't offer any other information and his manner was cold and gruff. I gave him my name and asked that he please let her know that I had called to say hello. He hung up so quickly that I couldn't be sure if he was going to deliver my message or if he had even stayed on the line long enough to hear me. I didn't call again after my second attempt, and consoled myself with the knowledge that within a week I would see her in class.

When I finally did get to see Gloria again, she seemed excited that I had tried to reach her and confirmed that her stepfather had never mentioned my calls. In what I considered an exceptional display of fair-mindedness on my part, I speculated that he might have forgotten.

"He didn't forget," she said angrily. She didn't say any more than that, but my attempts to call her had obviously made a favorable impression, as she now seemed to look forward to biology class and our chances to visit as much as I did. I didn't try jumping into deeply personal conversations immediately, but I did learn which days and times were best to call her home in order to reach her directly. All this created a sense of well-being in me, a belief that I would, in fact, find a way for us to be together. And then, in a continuance of my good fortune, before the month of January was over I got a part-time job as a short order cook at the Shadow Box restaurant.

The Shadow Box was located in the rear half of Keller's drug store on the northwest corner of Lake Street and Bloomington Avenue, within walking distance of our house. The restaurant seated up to one-hundred-fifty people and drew regular customers from the neighborhood and local businesses, as well as crowds from the nearby East Lake movie theater. The restaurant was managed for Mr. Keller by Jim and Beatrice Zena. Jim was the head cook, responsible for creating the menu, hiring kitchen help, ordering supplies and any other duties involved in running the kitchen. Bea managed the dining room and hired and supervised all the waitresses, busboys and fountain help. While much of my training as the new short order cook fell to one of Mr. Zena's other cooks, he also took time to personally ensure I was properly oriented to his expectations of the kitchen help.

I judged Mr. Zena to be considerably older than my father, but he insisted I refer to him as Jim. With a rather bulbous nose, a wreath of white hair no more substantial than dust and the grayest eyes I had ever seen, he vaguely reminded me of the entertainer Jimmy Durante. Despite his benign looks and chatty demeanor around the staff, Jim ran the kitchen with military discipline and displayed a fearsome temper when provoked by what he interpreted as incompetence or laziness. On more than one occasion I saw him drive waitresses to tears with no more than a withering look and an angry, pressured delivery of the words, "Get out of my sight."

I did my best to memorize the menu, follow instructions on how to keep the grills and deep fryers acceptably clean, arrange the steam table for lunches and dinners, prepare and keep track of multiple orders being grilled or fried and generally avoid any triggers to Jim's temper. I was determined to be successful in my first job. My pay was one dollar and twenty cents an hour and my initial schedule provided for twenty-two hours a week, including weekends. Not a bad start, I thought, toward independence and all those glittering prizes of my imagination.

While meal times were generally busy to the point of near chaos, the lulls between meals allowed for brief authorized breaks and the opportunity to clean the kitchen and restock whatever might be needed for the next meal. Reading or talking to the waitresses or generally goofing off between rushes was something Jim did not tolerate well. He and I often worked Sunday afternoons and evenings together and in mid-afternoon he would leave the kitchen for a brief nap in a lounge chair he kept in the basement stockroom. Upon his return he would check to see if I had completed whatever work had needed to be done in preparation for the Sunday dinner hour. It was during this quiet period when he returned from his rest and before the dinner hour that he often engaged me in conversations ranging in topics from sports to weather to religion. I listened closely to what he had to say and kept mostly silent whenever I found myself in disagreement.

A self-proclaimed fan of the University of Minnesota Gopher football team, he seemed constantly frustrated by their play and often turned off the radio he kept atop a butcher block in the corner of the kitchen long before the game had ended. He offered ongoing commentaries on the economy, local politics, sports and international issues. He was quick to offer his opinion that the revolutionary, Fidel Castro, who had overthrown the Cuban dictator, Batista, earlier in the month, was no freedom fighter at all, as so many people thought, but nothing more than "a lousy Commie thug." This seemed to mirror the opinion of my history teacher, though she had expressed her concerns in more subtle and diplomatic terms. But his favorite topics, once he learned that I was Catholic, appeared to be religion and life lessons he had learned. He had been raised a Catholic and had not "fallen away," he wanted me to know, but had very thoughtfully walked away.

"You know what never made any damned sense to me?" Jim said as he rolled back the covers on the steam table one Sunday afternoon and scanned the trays of dinner items being kept warm.

"No," I said, with no idea what was on his mind.

"That whole virgin birth thing. That never made a damned bit of sense to me."

"The virgin birth?"

"Yeah, Mary giving birth to Jesus and being a virgin, that never made any sense to me at all."

I wasn't sure how to respond, or even if I should respond to such an unexpected and intimate revelation of his beliefs.

He lifted the last cover and peered inside. "What time did you take the baked potatoes out of the oven?"

"Five o'clock," I said, relieved that he was now on a work topic.

"Good," he said as he closed the cover. "Yeah, that just never made any sense to me at all. I just couldn't believe it, even as a kid. I mean, how could a woman be a virgin and give birth? That's impossible."

He leaned against the steam table and stared at me, apparently waiting for my view on the issue.

"Well, I was taught it's a miracle," I began. "I mean, there are all sorts of miracles in the Bible, I don't suppose that one is really any more fantastic than any of the others. I suppose you either believe in them or you don't." I stopped there and hoped that my answer was neither antagonistic nor about to trigger any more of Jim's theological struggles.

"I could never believe it," he said, continuing to stare at me.

"Well," I said, and let the word fade into silence.

"Your folks ever tell you about the depression in the '30s?" he said, his arms were now folded across his chest, his gaze steady.

"Oh, yes. Yes, they sure have."

"Well, I'll tell you what, it taught me what really matters in this life." He reached into the left hip pocket of his steel-gray chef's pants and extracted his wallet. "Right here," he said, and shook the thick, leather wallet in my face, his jaw muscles tense. "The old bucks, that's what matters in this world."

"Well . . ."

He stuffed the wallet back into his hip pocket and slapped it twice for emphasis. "That's my god, right there—the old bucks."

To my great relief, one of the waitresses approached at that moment and laid an order slip on the counter of the window. Jim picked up the order, read it and handed it to me. "This is yours," he said.

I read the order and busied myself making the sandwiches written on the slip. A second waitress appeared and placed another slip on the counter. Jim read the order. "This is yours, too," he said and passed the order to me. He watched me for a moment, then turned and walked toward the far end of the steam table. "I'm going to grab a quick smoke before the rush, then I'll give you a hand."

"Okay, great," I said as he walked away.

While I focused on putting up the orders, I also thought about Jim and what he had said. I wondered why, out of all the extraordinary stories and miracles recorded in the Bible, his faith—or whatever faith he might once have had—reached some critical point of failure over the account of the virgin birth. After all, I thought, wasn't it as great a test of faith to believe that people could be healed of blindness by a touch, or that they could rise from the dead? Wasn't the miracle of loaves and fishes as equally astounding as the virgin birth? They were, in the end, all miracles. They all contradicted the laws of nature. It seemed so odd to me that he found this particular event to be the one that was just too outlandish and illogical to believe and had, ultimately, left him with an irreparably shattered faith. I wondered if it had something to do with the sexual nature of the miracle that I wasn't yet sophisticated enough to appreciate, which other adults would readily comprehend. "Ah yes," I could imagine some gray-bearded adult saying slyly, "that is, of course, by far the greatest single test of faith that we must ultimately confront." I was curious about the reasoning behind Jim's disbelief, but I was determined not to ask him about it.

    I believed he was sincere in what he had told me, including his pronouncement that money, or "the old bucks," as he put it, was his god. And yet, when he had made that statement, I felt that he wanted me to somehow challenge him. Before he had walked away to have his cigarette, there was a moment when I felt he wanted me to somehow assail the substance and validity of his proclaimed faith.

Eight

There was a reason for Tom's anger. From the time I had first known him, Tom had been in a constant struggle at home. His father, an unrepentant alcoholic, seemed to reserve his most extraordinary fits of meanness for Tom. The eldest of three children, it was Tom who incurred the wrath of their father when anything real or imagined went wrong in their home. It was Tom who was somehow to blame when his father was laid off from his job as an auto mechanic for over six months. It was Tom who was to blame whenever his younger brother and sister got into fights with each other. And it was Tom who was to blame when work was left undone around the house. The physical beatings he had endured as a child had begun to lessen in the past year or so, as Tom was clearly able to defend himself now—and might even present a serious threat to his father. His mother hovered somewhere in the background, a ghostly and colorless presence with no voice or energy to any longer be an influence within the home, someone consumed with laundry and meal preparation and who provided what care and protection she could for her children.

All this had left Tom with a clear understanding of life. The world was, at best, an indifferent place that would consume anyone not equal to its variety of assaults and challenges. There should be no expectation of kindness or understanding or sympathy. Life was most always brutal, where only the strong survived and weakness of any kind was the only real sin. And yet, I detected times when Tom allowed himself to believe, or at least hope, that there could be a more gentle way to exist. However fleeting, there were times when his youth still granted him some spark of hope that life might not necessarily be as dark and ruinous as he had been led to believe.

On most Friday evenings, Tom stopped in at the Shadow Box to see if I wanted to follow our usual routine and cruise Lake

Street for an hour or so, catch up on smoking cigarettes and maybe stop at Porky's for something to eat or drink. My shift on Friday evening was typically finished at nine o'clock, which left some time before I needed to be home to get some sleep before reporting back to work at eight o'clock Saturday morning. He would wait for me at the counter of the dining room while I finished up whatever orders I was working on, cleaned myself up a bit and changed clothes. On a Friday night late in January I had kept him waiting for more than a quarter of an hour and hurried to change once I was able to leave the kitchen.

When I got out to the counter, Tom seemed in no hurry to leave the restaurant and showed no irritation at my delay in finishing my shift. He was talking with one of the waitresses working the counter as I approached. "Sorry it took me so long to get out of there tonight," I said as I approached.

Tom said something to the waitress, and then swung on the stool to face in my direction. "Hey, no problem," he said with uncharacteristic pleasantness. He turned back to the waitress. "Nice talking to you. See you again."

I shouldered my way into my navy-blue tanker jacket as we headed out the back door to the parking lot and toward Tom's car. He had already lit up a cigarette before we reached the car. "What do you know about her?" he said.

"Cindy?"

"No, Marilyn Monroe. Yeah, Cindy, the little blonde I was talking to."

"Not much, really. She goes to Roosevelt. I think she might be a junior there, but I'm not sure. She's always real nice. She's a good waitress, hardly ever screws up an order."

Tom laughed. "Yeah, Will, I was hoping she was a good waitress."

"Hey, I'm just telling you what I know about her." I lit a cigarette and made several attempts to blow smoke rings and recover my aplomb as we headed east on Lake Street.

"She sure is a looker."

"Yeah, she's a cutie, no doubt about that."

"Is she going with anyone?"

"Not that I know of."

There was a brief pause before Tom spoke again. "You interested in her?"

I immediately thought of Gloria. I hadn't said anything to Tom, or really anyone other than Dee about my feelings for Gloria. "No, I'm not interested in her."

"You sure?"

"Yeah, I'm sure."

Tom drove on, the rear end of the Ford swaying from side to side on the icy street as he accelerated toward an amber light. He drove several blocks and past Pioneers and Soldiers Cemetery before he spoke again. "Man, she sure has a great body."

"Yeah," I said. I hated the expression. It always caused me to envision a headless cadaver lying somewhere on a cold, stone slab, but everyone used it and there was no point in complaining about it.

We made a right turn off Lake Street into Porky's parking lot. Tom hit a pothole composed of ice and slush at the entrance and the Ford jolted upward and then banged down hard as its front end cleared the hazard. Tom didn't react, which I took as a measure of how deeply he was in thought about Cindy. As we searched for a parking space, a Chevy coupe suddenly backed out of its space and into our path. There was no blasting of the horn or shouting from Tom, not even a wrathful finger held out the window toward the driver of the Chevy. "I think I might ask her out," he said at last. "What do you think?"

"Sure," I said, "why not?"

"Yeah," he said, "I should ask her out. I mean, what the hell."

I had never seen Tom so tentative. "Maybe I could find a girl to ask out too and we could double."

"Yeah," Tom said immediately. "That's a good idea. Four of us could go out together. That would be good."

"There's a place over on Chicago Avenue just off Lake Street where they hold dances every weekend. It might be a good place for a first date."

Tom exhaled a long stream of smoke out his nose, rolled down his window and flipped the cigarette butt outside. "Yeah, I don't know. I'm not much of a dancer."

"I don't think it's a big deal. You just wait for the slow songs. Hold her close and kind of sway around the room."

"Yeah, well, I'm thinking maybe we could just go to a movie and get something to eat afterward."

"Sure, that's good too."

Tom leaned back in his seat and grew silent. When he spoke again his enthusiasm seemed dimmed and tempered by whatever thoughts stirred behind his downcast eyes. "I don't know. We'll see how it goes. We might be getting way ahead of ourselves, Will. I'll have to talk to her some more, maybe get some idea if she'd even consider going out with me."

"Sure," I said, "I understand. Well, just let me know."

"I tell you what," he said, brightening again, "if you see me out there talking to her, don't be in a big hurry to finish up your shift. You can take your sweet time, 'cause she's a lot nicer to look at than you." He leaned toward me and punched me in the shoulder.

"No argument there."

Nine

THE BEST TIMES TO REACH GLORIA on the phone were Tuesday and Wednesday evenings after six o'clock. I usually worked at the restaurant on Wednesday evenings, so that only left Tuesdays. I took advantage of the time to talk with her, bolting down my dinner and calling each Tuesday evening at a minute or two after six if the phone was available to me. I saw her in biology too, and I followed Dee's advice to remain patient. Our conversations were wide-ranging, covering everything from classes to movies to friends to music to our most deeply held hopes. I loved talking with her and the hour or so faded too quickly before I found myself waiting until the next time that we could talk. Everything seemed secondary to seeing her face and her smile and hearing her voice. As soon as I woke each morning, she was in my thoughts. My days were marked by exquisite anticipation, as if I were now seeing the world through new eyes.

I told her about my new job and my boss and his strange and varied revelations. I told her about my goal of eventually buying a car of my own and how much I regretted that I had no means at present to take her out on a proper date. As Dee had predicted, Gloria explained that I didn't need to own a car in order for us to spend time together. She would be more than happy to walk or take a bus to a movie or a restaurant or just walk and talk. We only needed to find opportunities when we could spend time together, she said, and a car really wasn't that important. I was, of course, happy that she felt as she did, but I knew a car would provide us a degree of freedom that we could never experience otherwise, and my ambition was only strengthened by my desire to be with her. I told her about Tom's interest in one of the waitresses at the Shadow Box and the idea that we might double date if things worked out for him. Gloria thought that would be fun, but explained again that I shouldn't be concerned about having a car.

We agreed that my new job had the undesirable consequence of allowing even fewer hours for us to get together, and that our situation would likely worsen in March when Gloria turned sixteen and hoped to find a job, too. We would, no doubt, both be working weekends and several nights a week. She thought about applying for work at the Shadow Box, where we could work together, but she lived much closer to the White Castle and it looked unlikely that we would be hiring new staff over the next several months. Nevertheless, we would find a way to be together.

Despite my new job and my obsession with Gloria, my classes were going well enough, and geometry provided an inglorious opportunity to secure whatever grade I might want. Mr. Horton, a gray-haired, scowling veteran of high school academia, taught geometry in near absentia. He began each class announcing what chapters we needed to read and what practice problems we needed to work on, and then, many days, left the room for the remainder of the hour. He at times asked if anyone had any questions, but his demeanor seemed to make that offer more of a challenge than an opportunity and was rarely met with any takers. He didn't gather practice sheets and we were allowed to correct our own quizzes. We didn't need to show any work on our examinations and simply turned in the test sheet showing our answers and the number of items we found to be correct. I made a fairly ambitious effort to learn geometry by simply reading the text and working on the practice problems as instructed, but it wasn't long before I was struggling to tutor myself through the subject and decided that I would, if necessary, use the self-scoring means of escape that was obviously available to us.

This was the one class I shared with Junior Kandowski, who was seated several rows to my right. On a Thursday early in February, while students were still talking about the death of Buddy Holly, Ritchie Valens and the Big Bopper in a plane crash in Iowa earlier in the week, Junior decided to question Mr. Horton's teaching technique. His request was honest and direct, with evidence only of frustration and not of disrespect. Mr. Horton had given us a reading assignment and was about to leave the room when Junior raised his hand.

"James, do you have a question?"

"Yes, Mr. Horton. I'm having a really difficult time following some of the text and understanding the problems. I don't know about the other students, but I could sure use some explanations of this stuff, especially the problems in chapter seven."

Mr. Horton stared at Junior for several seconds. His cheeks grew flushed as his head began to display a slight tremor. "That's not a question, James. Is there something specific that you don't understand?"

Junior remained calm. "I just think we could use more help with this stuff. I've tried to read it on my own but I don't think I'm really learning it as well as I could if you'd spend more time working the problems with us."

Mr. Horton turned away from the class and walked back behind his desk. He picked up the geometry text and held it out toward Junior as if he were brandishing a sword. "If you have a question about one of the problems, Mr. Kandowski, I would be happy to answer it." His voice boomed, clearly full of anger.

Junior seemed uncertain as to what he should do or say. "I just . . . I think we maybe aren't learning this very well."

Mr. Horton slammed the book down on top of his desk and the entire class jumped to what sounded like a rifle shot. "And just why should I care if you people learn anything?" Silence. "Why should I care?"

I couldn't believe what I heard and from the stark expression of shock on Junior's face, he was equally dumbfounded by what Mr. Horton had said. I watched Junior, as did every other student in the class. It seemed clear he wasn't about to pursue his line of questioning any further.

Mr. Horton took several steps toward Junior. He pushed his suit coat back and placed his hands on his hips, arms akimbo, his head thrust forward. "You people want to know something?" His voice was pressured and quavered with emotion. "This school is set up with about eighty percent college preparatory classes and twenty percent shop classes, and it ought to be just the other way around. Most of you people are not going to be going on to college. That's right: I said you are not going to college." He paused, evidently to let that piece of information settle into our consciousnesses. "You're going to be working in factories or on assembly lines. You're going to be in the same sort of jobs your parents have. If you think I'm wrong about that, just take a look at some of your former classmates here at South and see where they are today."

He stopped speaking, but stood and stared at Junior. His head shook from side to side and his cheeks were now nearly crimson. The room was eerily silent and seemed to me to have grown extraordinarily warm. I suspected that we were all speechless with both fear of causing an even greater display of his temper and bewilderment and despair at his devastating indictment of our collective future. As he stood and glared at us, I couldn't help but wonder what personal history had brought him to this moment and this undisguised anger with us. He said nothing further, but turned and walked out of the classroom and slammed the door. He didn't return until the hour was nearly over some twenty minutes later. During the time he was gone not one of us spoke. When he returned his hostility appeared unabated. He waited until the bell rang to announce that we were to read the first half of chapter eight for next week and then stood near the door and watched each student as they left the room.

I caught up with Junior in the hallway. "What the hell was that all about?"

Junior continued to hurry down the corridor, but turned to look at me. His face was a graphic mixture of anger and hurt. "I don't know," he said. "That guy just frustrates the hell out of me. I just might see if I can get transferred to another class."

"Man, I never saw the guy so mad. I thought for a second he was going to take a swing at you. It was pretty damned scary."

Junior stopped walking and turned to look at me again. "I'll tell you something, Will. I'm not going to let him decide who I am or what I will become. No way does he get to decide that."

Ten

JUNIOR STAYED IN MR. HORTON'S CLASS. The only real change was that Junior began to ask specific questions of Mr. Horton, frequently approaching his desk with his text and quietly and calmly asking if he could go over a problem with him. Mr. Horton's response was unexpectedly friendly and helpful, and often he would approach the blackboard and show Junior how to work the problem in question. There was no evidence of his previous antipathy toward Junior or the class. And though he made no apology for his past outburst, I suspected that he felt some degree of remorse for what he had said.

Tom continued to engage Cindy in long conversations each Friday evening, while I delayed finishing my shift as long as I could. For reasons Tom couldn't or wouldn't share with me, he kept putting off asking her out on a date as the weeks hurried on toward spring. It was a bit of a mystery to me, and I think it mystified Cindy, too. Whenever I approached the subject of why he still hadn't asked her out he cut me off with abrupt answers that told me nothing. "I will, just leave it alone," he'd say, or "Give it a rest. I'll let you know when I've asked her." His hesitancy was an ongoing disappointment to both Cindy and me, and eventually Cindy asked me if I thought Tom wanted to date her. "I'm pretty sure he does," I said, "I guess he's just shier than I realized."

Gloria and I continued to search for any time when we could talk or see each other, and then, unexpectedly, there was an opportunity to be together—alone. On a Friday in late March in biology class, Gloria told me that the following Tuesday evening she would be home without her mother or stepfather. She invited me to her house and assured me that she would be alone from six until sometime around ten o'clock. I promised her that I would be at her house as soon as possible after I had finished dinner. The thought of spending time alone with her was so exciting as to be nearly unbearable and I found myself unable to think about much else in the days leading up to Tuesday evening.

I tried not to swallow my dinner in a single bite, but strained to pace myself and then declined dessert. I waited a few minutes before slipping on my tanker jacket and heading toward the door.

"Will, where are you headed in such a hurry?" Mom asked as I headed out the door.

"I need to stop over at Gloria Jensen's house, Mom. We have a biology project we need to discuss. Her place is less than a mile away and I promised I'd stop over." There was no current biology project, but at least the destination was accurate.

Mom hesitated a moment. "Well, not too late. I'm sure you have other homework to do and you've got work tomorrow night."

"I'll be home no later than nine, I promise."

The day had been unusually warm and the streets and sidewalks were lined and dotted with slush from the melting snow that was now beginning to refreeze in the early evening cold. I could see spiderwebs of ice crystals forming on shallow puddles as I hurried down Cedar Avenue, my feet seeming to barely touch the ground. I tried to smell my own breath by holding the heel of my hand on my chin and exhaling into my palm and cupped fingers to direct my breath toward my nose. I couldn't smell a thing. Then, unexpectedly, I felt a point of soreness on the tip of my nose. No doubt I was in the process of sprouting a pimple in the very center of my face. I tested the spot with my index finger. It felt like it had potential to become a colossal embarrassment over the next day or two. If only it would remain subdued for the next several hours. I could hear Tom's voice calling me "Will the Worrier," and tried to stop thinking about anything other than getting to Gloria's house. *How about "Tom the Timid,"* I thought, and again resented his failure to ask Cindy out on a date.

It was nearly seven o'clock when I got to Gloria's house. The front door opened just as I was about to knock. Gloria stepped back as she swung the door open. She was wearing a pink V-neck sweater and blue jeans and holding a gray tabby cat in one arm. With her free hand, she brushed her hair back behind her left ear. "Hi, Will. Come in, come in." she said in a single breath

I stepped into the small entryway and took off my shoes. Placing them in a rubber boot tray off to the right side, I slipped off my tanker jacket and hung it on one of the hooks above the boot tray. "I got here as fast as I could. I'm supposed to be back home by nine."

"Okay. Well, at least we have a couple of hours to ourselves," she said. There was a long silence and with her words I suddenly felt both the incredible exhilaration and full weight of our meeting. I hadn't really thought about just exactly what I would do once we were alone together, and the reality created a tension I suspected neither of us had previously felt or anticipated. "This is Josephine," she said, and with a two-fingered grasp, waved one of the tabby's paws at me.

"Hi, Josephine," I said as sweetly as I could and then reached out to pet her. Josephine recoiled like a cobra about to strike and issued a threatening hiss. I pulled my hand back. "That can't be a good start," I said.

"Josephine, no! This is Will, a good guy." She put the cat on the floor. "I'll put her down in the basement. She doesn't really know any men other than Martin, so she probably thinks any male is a jerk. I'll be right back," she said as she shooed the cat along.

"Martin?"

"My stepfather."

"Oh, right," I said. "You sure seem to hate that guy." Gloria didn't respond, but silently herded the cat toward the back of the house and down a flight of stairs into the basement. I immediately regretted saying anything about her stepfather, the one topic that drove some mysterious wedge between us.

Gloria closed the door to the basement and came back toward the entryway. "Come in, Will. I can give you the grand tour if want." My reference to her stepfather had evidently taken a momentary toll on her mood, but she seemed to recover quickly.

I stepped into the living room. "Sure, whatever you'd like." I looked around the room. There was a television on the wall to my left, with a couch on the opposite wall and a single overstuffed chair in a corner. A small coffee table made of highly polished driftwood sat in front of the couch. Beyond the living room was a dining room and beyond that a kitchen. Gloria pointed all this out without moving from the spot where she stood, motioning like a traffic cop to various points of the house. To the left of the dining room and through a small archway was the bathroom, flanked by bedrooms on either side. The bedroom toward the back of the house was Gloria's, and her mom and Martin occupied the front bedroom. "It's a lot like our place," I said. I had no idea what to do or say next. I couldn't believe how awkward I now felt around the girl I had come to know so well over the preceding months. It was as if being alone with her created a new and unexplored territory of our friendship, filled with anxiety and a self-conscious uncertainty.

"Would you like a Coke or something?"

"Sure. That would be great." As the two of us headed toward the kitchen, I wanted to take her by the shoulders, turn her toward me and kiss her until she was breathless, but I suspected that would spoil everything. Or maybe that was exactly what she would like me to do. Who really knew about girls?

"Do you like some of the western shows on television?" she said as she poured Coke for both of us.

"Sure."

"*Sugarfoot* is on right now, do you ever watch that?"

"Yeah, I love *Sugarfoot*. Good old Tom Brewster and his goofy sidekick Toothy Thompson."

"Why don't we take these into the living room and watch some television?"

"Great," I said, probably with a little too much enthusiasm.

* * * * *

*S*UGARFOOT WAS NEARLY HALF OVER when I finally put my left arm across Gloria's shoulders in the darkened living room. To my relief, she didn't protest, but leaned in against my left side. I could feel the warmth of her body through her sweater and jeans and smell a hint of sweet, soapy freshness as she nestled against me. I could feel my face flush with excitement. A desire to kiss her swept over me again, but I decided to wait a little longer. I debated whether I should ask her or simply make a move. I watched *Sugarfoot* for several more minutes, completely unaware of the plot of the story unfolding on the TV screen. Finally, I turned toward her, "Gloria?"

She looked up at me, her face smooth as ivory and hauntingly beautiful in the flickering glow from the television. "Mmmm?" she murmured and smiled at me.

I pulled her close and kissed her. Her lips were soft and warm and responsive. I thought kissing her might be awkward, but it wasn't. She reached up with one hand and grasped me behind the back of my neck and pulled me closer to her. The thrill was even greater than I had anticipated and I felt my heart beating like mad and an uncontrollable tumescence as she turned toward me and pressed one of her legs against my thigh. My breath came more quickly and I pulled back to look at her. "Gloria," I said, not knowing what to do or say next.

"Don't talk," she said, "just hold me close." She leaned back into the length of the couch and pulled me down with her. I thought I saw tears gathering in her eyes, but it was difficult to know in the darkness and it made no sense to me, so I simply lowered my head to kiss her again. I felt the cool, moist spillage of tears on her cheeks as I kissed her. "What's wrong, Gloria? Did I do something wrong? What did I do?"

"Nothing. Don't talk. Just kiss me."

"Why are you crying? Something must be wrong."

She smiled. "I'm not crying and there's nothing wrong. It's just . . . I've wanted you to kiss me for a long time. Did you know that?"

"No. I mean, I hoped, but I didn't know for sure." I wanted to tell her I loved her, but it seemed to go wildly beyond whatever point we were at in our relationship and I was afraid it would spoil the moment, and yet I did believe I loved her. *This must be what love feels like,* I thought. I waited a few seconds and then leaned forward to kiss her again.

She pushed me back gently, her hands against my shoulders. "I trust you, Will. I feel that I can trust you more than anyone I've ever known. And that's the most important thing in the world to me. Do you understand?"

It seemed to me such an odd and unexpected thing for her to say. I wondered what thoughts and memories moved her at that moment, what reflections took place behind that beautiful face that smiled at me, tear-stained and mysterious in the shifting light.

"Yes," I said, and wiped the tears from her cheeks.

Eleven

"Yes, sir, Bea and I never had any kids. You know, a lot of people bring kids into this world and can't provide for them, can't take care of them at all. Then, because they don't have any money or brains, they end up drinking and fighting with each other and the kids suffer and the whole damned family falls apart. You see it all the time. They're just thinking about themselves—or they're not thinking at all, just want to have sex and then end up with kids they didn't want." Jim took off his paper overseas-style cook's hat and used the sleeve of his chef's jacket to wipe beads of sweat from his forehead. He put his hat back on, leaned forward and put his elbows against the counter window that looked out toward the dining room. "Yeah, it's a hell of a world to bring kids into."

Jim had decided to skip his afternoon nap on this particular Sunday, which allowed more time for his kitchen ruminations. Since Jim and Beatrice were clearly making substantial money managing the restaurant, I could only assume they had decided against having children only because, as he stated, it was a hell of a world. I let his observations pass without comment.

A waitress came to the window, dropped an order on the counter and smiled at Jim. "Here you go," she said.

"I'm not going anywhere," Jim growled at her as he picked up the slip. He read the order and then handed it to me. "This is yours."

I threw a hamburger patty on the grill and dropped one of the baskets of raw cut French fries into the smaller of two deep fryers. Jim turned toward me and leaned back against the serving board of the steam table and crossed his arms. "Did I tell you that Bea and I got a color television?"

"No, you didn't."

"Yeah, we've had it a few weeks now. We love it. Not all your shows are in color, of course, but they will be someday. You can bet on that."

"I suppose they will."

Jim didn't say anything immediately and I began to wonder if he had read some sort of insult into my response, or thought I was somehow making fun of him. I had learned that Jim was more than a little sensitive, if not floridly paranoid.

"Yup, the color is just great. Looks just like you were there. Have you seen any color TV?"

"Just models in the stores."

"Oh, I tell you, it's terrific."

I began to wish more orders would show up in the window as I flipped the burger and did a quick check on the progress of the fries. You never knew what unpredictable and dangerous avenues Jim's conversations might pursue.

"You ever watch *The Perry Como Show*?"

"Sure. Well, mostly my parents watch his show."

"That's in color. You can see Perry and all his guests in color. You just wait. Pretty soon most of your shows will be in color."

"That's great."

He continued to watch me work on the order without further comment. "Yeah, well maybe sometime you can come over and watch a show with Bea and me."

I was shocked. I couldn't imagine what must have caused him to extend such an invitation. "Yeah, maybe we could do that sometime."

"Well, you're not too busy here at the moment. I'm going to grab a cigarette before the dinner rush starts. If you start getting swamped, just give me a holler. Matt will be coming on in half an hour too, not that he's a real big help," he said, referring to Matt Patrick, a middle-aged man of a somewhat simple nature whose duties as a cook were not much greater than mine and who had evidently disappointed Jim in not learning more about managing the kitchen.

"Okay, Jim. Hey, and thanks for the invitation."

"Yeah, yeah. I'm gonna grab a smoke now."

* * * * *

The dinner hour was unusually busy and by the time my shift was coming to an end I had been on my feet for nearly five straight hours. It was almost seven o'clock when one of the new waitresses stuck her head into the order window, frowned at me and said, "There's some guy out here wants to talk to you."

"Who is it?"

"I don't know. I ain't your secretary."

"Charming," I said when she was out of earshot. I looked toward the archway that opened up to the dining room. I saw Tom standing near the entrance, looking as though he might enter the kitchen area. I put down the order I was working on and started to walk around the steam table and out of the kitchen.

"Where you headed?" Jim asked. His voice hovered between incredulity and anger.

"I have to talk to a friend of mine for just a second. I'll be right back."

Tom looked troubled and uncertain, his shoulders uncharacteristically slumped forward, his face pale. "Shit, Tom, you shouldn't have come back in here," I said as I tried to maneuver him away from the entrance to the kitchen and Jim's line of sight.

"Is Cindy working tonight?"

"No, she usually doesn't work on Sundays. Is that all?"

"What time are you off? I'll give you a ride home."

"I'm done in fifteen minutes. Just go sit in one of the booths and get something to drink. I'll be back in a little bit. And don't ever step back in this area, Tom, my boss goes nuts. If you need to see me or talk to me, just tell one of the waitresses, but don't walk back into the kitchen area."

"Yeah, sorry," he said faintly.

"Just go sit somewhere, Tom. Don't mess this up for me."

He turned away and raised one hand to signal his agreement with my demand. "I'm cool."

I headed back to the kitchen under Jim's intense, gray-eyed gaze. "I don't want any of your buddies walking back in here like this is some kind of pool hall or something. Nobody's allowed in the kitchen area but employees. Nobody."

"I told him he couldn't be back here. He just didn't know. It won't ever happen again."

"It better not," Jim said. I assumed my job was probably safe but my invitation to watch his color television set, I thought, had likely been withdrawn.

* * * * *

T<small>OM WAS HOVERING OVER A CUP</small> of hot chocolate when I joined him in one of the booths. His face was slumped forward over his drink. One of the overhead lights penetrated his close-cropped hair, revealing a pinkish scalp.

I flopped into the brown vinyl bench-seat across from him. "What's up, Tom?"

"I thought maybe you might want to head over to Beek's for some pizza before you go home."

"I'm not really hungry. Working around food all day kind of takes your appetite away. Besides, that's not what I meant. You seem upset about something—and I know you didn't come here just to check on whether or not Cindy was working."

Tom looked up. His brow was furrowed and he clenched his teeth, causing the muscles to flex in the corners of his jaw. "That reminds me, I'm definitely asking her out the next time I see her. No more hesitation—you'll see."

I waited but he didn't say anything more. "Tom, what's going on? Something's on your mind."

"Ah, just a shit night in a long string of shit nights."

"Yeah, so what happened?"

One of the night crew waitresses came to the table before Tom could answer. "You want anything, Will?"

"Just a small Coke. Thanks, Shirley."

"You got it," she said as she walked away.

Tom waited until she was ostensibly beyond hearing range. "I kind of had it out with my old man tonight. It got uglier than it ever has before. I came this close," he held up his right hand, thumb and index finger a fraction of an inch apart, "to knocking him on his ass."

"Man, Tom, what happened?"

Tom swirled the remains of his hot chocolate around in the bottom of his cup and waited until Shirley placed the Coke on the table and again retreated. He leaned forward and lowered his voice. "He was drunk, as usual, and had been yelling at my mom all night. I don't even know what the hell it was about. Shit, with him it doesn't have to be about anything. Anyway, I was trying to watch something on TV and the yelling in the kitchen starts getting so bad that I tell my brother and sister to just stay out of the way and I'll see what's going on. I get back in the kitchen and he's got Mom backed into a corner. He's got his hand in the air like he's going to slap her or something. I just fucking exploded."

I looked around quickly to see if anyone had heard Tom. Fortunately, the restaurant was mostly empty. "Hey, take it easy with the language."

Tom was caught up in his story now and didn't seem to hear me. "I grabbed the son of a bitch and swung him around and told him if he wanted to hit someone to try taking a swing at me." He stopped for a moment and took a deep breath.

"God, Tom. Has he ever hit her before?"

"Not in front of me, but who knows? And lately he's been getting worse, some shit about trouble with his boss at the garage. There's always some damned excuse."

"So what happened?"

Tom raised his head and looked at me directly. "He backed off. I could see in his eyes that he wasn't going to swing on me. It's the first time in my life that I actually saw the guy look a little scared. I guess I must have had one nasty-ass look on my face. I think he could see that I wasn't bluffing—and I wasn't." He laughed, but it was a humorless laugh. I took it to be more an expression of thinly veiled despair than anything else, and I believe if he hadn't laughed he would have wept.

"What's going on there now? I mean, is your mom okay?"

Tom lowered his head again and stared into his empty cup. "Yeah, she'll be okay. Dad swore a couple of times under his breath and then stumbled out of the kitchen and went into his bedroom and slammed the door. He'll sleep it off tonight."

"Man, Tom, that's really bad." I didn't know what more to say. I had known for years that Tom's father drank too much and had never shown Tom any discernable kindness, but this confrontation had elevated the tension between the two of them to a new level. "Did you ever think of calling the cops when he gets like that?"

"Cops, shit," he said with disgust. "They'd come over and he'd talk his way out of it and my mom would back everything he'd say. And when they left he'd probably beat the crap out of her. There's only one thing he understands, and that's someone in the home standing up to him and letting him know he's going to get as good as he gives. Believe me, Will, it's the only way to stop the guy."

All I could think about was that I was lucky not to live in a home like Tom's. Maybe my father wasn't the warmest and most understanding guy who ever lived, and at times his taciturn anger about most things drove me to despair, but I couldn't imagine him ever raising his hand to my mother.

"Hey, Will, don't start worrying for me," he said and reached across the table to take a half-hearted punch at my shoulder. "Why don't the two of us go over to Beek's Pizza and kill an hour or two? I feel like I need to unwind."

Given what had happened at his home and the mood he was in, I felt it was better than an even chance that he would find someone in Beek's who would become the target of his suppressed fury. "I really just want to head home tonight. I've been on my feet all day."

"You sure?"

"Yeah, I'm sure. Maybe another time."

"Okay. I'll give you a ride. Hey," he said as he began to slide out of the booth, "I'm coming in next Friday and asking Cindy out."

"Great," I said as the two of us got up from the booth and headed toward the back door and the parking lot. Tom was just a step or two behind me.

"Yeah, I figure if things work out really well I can bring her over to my house for dinner some night and she can meet the whole family."

That's it, I thought. That's why he had continually put off asking her out. "You know, Tom, she'd be dating you, not your family or your old man."

"Yeah, right, Will. She probably lives in some starry dreamland, but hey, we'll see how it goes."

Twelve

TWO DAYS BEFORE THE SCHOOL YEAR was to end, someone slashed all four tires on Mr. Horton's car while it was parked in the school lot. The rumor among the students was that Jim Scadola, a junior and former student of Mr. Horton's, had done it. It made sense to me. Scadola had had several famous run-ins with Mr. Horton, and Scadola wanted a reputation as a badass more than anything in the world. Despite general belief in the guilt of Scadola, evidently no one volunteered anything to the administration and no one was accused of the criminal damage before the school year ended. I couldn't help but think back to Junior's encounter with Mr. Horton and how this attack on his car must have once again confirmed every suspicion he had ever held about the vile worthlessness of the student body.

Tom had kept his word and taken Cindy out on two dates as summer vacation began. On the first date, he and Cindy went out for pizza and a double feature at the East Lake Theater. He had decided it would be better to wait until after the first date to see if we might double. While he didn't give me much detail about his date with her, he did mention that one of the movies was *King Creole* with Elvis Presley and said it provided the opportunity for him to get close to her. That piece of information was delivered with a wink and a punch to the shoulder. I didn't ask what that meant. At work, Cindy seemed happy about their date and told the other waitresses she had gone out with Tom. Their second date was a double date with Gloria and me.

The four of us went to a drive-in featuring a "triple monster night" with Frankenstein, Dracula and one of the old werewolf movies. We stayed for the first feature and then headed back to an A&W root beer stand on the corner of Lake Street and the river road.

Tom hadn't said anything to me, but I suspected after root beers he might look for a romantic place to park along the river road, perched somewhere high above the heavily treed, moonlit river valley. If that was the plan, it got subverted by Gloria's need to be home no later than midnight. She was apologetic, but said there was really nothing she could do about her curfew. Tom seemed disappointed but didn't badger her about staying out any later. And so we left the root beer stand and headed home along the river road, through the corridor of newly leafed trees, the moon shining through the windshield and an early spring breeze drifting in the windows, the car radio turned low as the music escaped into the night.

Our double date had gone well enough, I thought. Gloria and Cindy seemed to like each other and even had one of those prolonged girl conferences in the restroom of the drive-in, and Gloria was clearly disappointed that she needed to end our evening together. But I had detected some awkwardness in Tom that went beyond the usual nervousness of the early stages of dating. It was hard to define or quantify. There was something about his manner when he was around Cindy that seemed artificial and sadly contrived—as though he had been forced for so long to play the role of a tough guy that he could no longer find his way back to the innocent and unguarded boy he once had been. Gloria seemed to notice it too, even though she hadn't previously spent any time around Tom. And I understood her vague reference to his behavior when we arrived at her house.

I walked Gloria to her door. I wanted to kiss her goodnight but had an overpowering feeling that we were being watched, so I simply held both her hands as we said goodbye.

"I had a great time tonight, Will. I really like your friends, even though Tom seems to be sort of a nervous guy."

"I had a great time too," I said, and ignored her remark about Tom. "Maybe we could do it again sometime."

"That would be great," she said, and made no move to go into her house. As she prolonged the moment, I thought again about kissing her goodnight. And then I heard a doorknob turn and the creak of the door as it opened just a crack.

I squeezed both her hands. "Goodnight, Gloria. I'll talk to you soon."

"Goodnight, Will. Thanks again," she said and squeezed my hands in return.

* * * * *

A**ND SO SUMMER WAS OFF** to a promising start. I had to work full-time at the restaurant, and there were always chores to do at home, but I managed to find time to get to the beach at Lake Nokomis on occasion and see or talk to Gloria at least once or twice a week. Dee was home for the summer and was working, too. Mom had gotten her a job at the dress shop and she was evidently showing a great deal of skill as a sales clerk. Don, Dee's boyfriend from Duluth, was able to visit once in mid-June, spending most of a Sunday afternoon with us. I liked him immediately. He was tall, blond and still somewhat gangly even at his advanced age of twenty-two years. He looked at me directly when I spoke to him and he listened closely to whatever was said. Dad seemed to like him too, as he spent half an hour or more showing him every tool in our garage—an unmistakable sign of acceptance. Dee was visibly happy with the family's reaction to Don, though I believe it was of no surprise to her at all.

The Fourth of July fell on a Saturday and I wanted to take Gloria to the fireworks at Powderhorn Park, just a few blocks south of the restaurant. At first it looked as though that was going to be impossible, as I was scheduled to work an evening shift and help close the kitchen at ten. Gloria wasn't working that night and had offered to meet me at the Shadowbox, if I was able to take the night off. She said she could get a ride to the restaurant from one of her girlfriends and that after the fireworks we could grab a bus back toward our homes if we decided it was too far to walk. I was anxious to spend the evening with her. I told her I would ask Jim if I could get off early.

Typically, once Jim had made out a weekly schedule, nothing short of a national emergency could cause him to make a change—and he didn't care much for such requests from any of his employees. And so it was with a fair amount of trepidation that I asked nearly a week in advance if I might get off a couple of hours early on the fourth. His initial response was unequivocal. "You're scheduled to close that night," he said incredulously, as if my question sprang from some unfathomable ignorance on my part. I hesitated to ask again, knowing how Jim could publicly humiliate an employee who pushed a point too far. And then, on the Wednesday before the fourth, he stopped me just as I was about to leave the kitchen at the end of my shift.

"Do you still want to get off early on Saturday?" he said.

I sensed that he was about to grant my earlier request, but I couldn't imagine why. "Yeah, I really would."

"I understand you'd like to take some young lady to the fireworks at Powderhorn."

I felt a smoldering anger suddenly mix with my hopefulness. It seemed nothing was secret or private among the restaurant staff. "Yeah, I was hoping that we could go together if I could just get off by around seven or so."

Jim grinned. "What's the young lady's name?"

"Gloria. I know her from school."

"I see," Jim said, his grin widening just a bit. "Well, I tell you what, I think I can stick around that night and help Matt close the place. Bea and I are too old for fireworks and I really don't have anything planned for the night."

I couldn't believe my luck. Jim never worked late and more often than not didn't work at all on holidays. "Oh, thank you so much, Jim," I replied. "You just made my whole week."

Jim's grin broke into one of his rare, generous smiles. He slapped me on the back. "You're welcome. I guess you better run along now."

I started down the steps to the basement to change clothes when Jim called out to me. "Just a minute," he said and motioned me back up the steps. "I thought maybe you could use a few bucks, maybe buy her a pop or something." Jim pulled out his wallet and fished out three dollars. "Here, take this for the fourth. You and your Gloria have a good time."

"Well, I don't know . . . I mean, I really shouldn't."

"Go on, go on and take it," he said with feigned anger as he waved the money under my nose.

I took the bills from him. "Thank you so much, Jim. I don't know what else to say."

"Yeah, you don't need to say anything. Just have a good time and treat your girl right."

I started back down the steps. "Thanks again for the time off—and for the money." Jim just waved me off and headed back toward the steam table and the kitchen. I was nearly halfway down the steps to the basement when I thought to myself that Jim had just given me a little piece of his god. It seemed a rather odd thought that simply materialized of its own volition, but I liked the idea that, in fact, it was exactly what he'd done.

* * * * *

GLORIA WAS WAITING FOR ME in the restaurant dining room when I finished work at seven on the evening of the fourth. She wore light blue shorts and a loose, cream-colored cotton blouse that didn't fail to flatter her and tantalize me when she turned a certain way or was caressed by a warm July breeze. She had brought a small blanket for us to sit on at the fireworks, which I kept tucked under my left arm as we walked to the park, my right arm draped casually across her waist.

There was a small carnival near the old, gray stucco pavilion on the south end of the park's little lake. The tiny amber lights that outlined and defined the rides were already turned on by the time we reached the carnival. The aroma of hot dogs and cotton candy and popcorn filled the night air and it was exciting to hear the machines running and the shouts and screams of the patrons as they whirled and dipped and twisted in the gathering darkness. Gloria and I each had a Coke and then waited in a short line to ride the Tilt-A-Whirl. As our car swung in circles, rising and falling within the rotating platform, I felt the warmth and weight of our bodies forced against each other and I could only think about how much

I wanted to hold her in my arms and how kissing her was no longer nearly enough to satisfy my passion for her.

We took a second ride on the Tilt-A-Whirl and walked around the carnival grounds for a short time before we headed toward the grassy slope just to the west of the pavilion to search for a spot to watch the fireworks. The hillside faced the lake and a little island from which the fireworks would be launched. The grassy amphitheater was already swarming with people seeking an optimal vantage point. Children ran between blankets and lawn chairs and the slower-moving adults, waving sparklers and firing cap guns at each other as parents tried in vain to herd them onto whatever tiny plot of the hillside they had claimed for the night's entertainment. Gloria and I found an open area about halfway up the hill and spread our blanket out. Gloria sat on the blanket and pulled her knees up toward her chin as I stood looking down at her. "Do you want anything? I can run back down to the ride area and get us some Cracker Jacks or pop, if you want."

She looked up and smiled at me, her face bright and shiny like a child's in the fading light. "No thanks, Will. Just sit here with me and we'll wait for the fireworks."

I sat down beside her and put my arm across her back. She grabbed my hand and pulled it to her lips and kissed my palm. "I love the fireworks, don't you?"

"Yes."

"And I love being here with you."

By the time the fireworks began, I was resting my head in Gloria's lap as she slowly ran her fingers along my eyebrows and forehead. For half an hour or more, we watched with a thousand others as the night sky was illuminated with bursts of blue and green and gold light. When one of the rockets exploded into two or three successive canopies of cascading, shimmering colors, I could feel Gloria's legs wiggle with excitement and hear her join the throng in a breathless response of "Ooh." The finale to the display was a series of booming salutes that shook the island and the surrounding hillsides, followed by an upright, brilliant firework quilt of the American flag that stood out on the tip of the island.

The crowd rose and applauded. As the smoking flag began to sputter and fade away, people gathered up their blankets and chairs and began walking up or down the hillside to head home. We sat unmoving as the crowd dispersed all around us. "Do you want to walk along the lake? We can head over to Bloomington Avenue and catch the bus when we get to the other side of the park," I offered.

"Yes, that would be nice," she said, "but I hate that it's over."

We sauntered down the hill and began to follow the sidewalk around the lake. As we neared the spot where the walk curved away from the lake, just before we were exposed to the halo of a corner streetlight, I took Gloria in my arms and wrapped the blanket over our shoulders like a giant serape. I pulled her close and kissed her and felt her body relax into mine. I could hear her breathing quicken. I moved my right hand experimentally toward her breast.

"Oh, Will," she whispered, as she pushed my hand away, "Please don't do that. Please."

"Gloria," I said, "there's nothing wrong with it." It sounded trite and foolish and untrue, even as I spoke the words. I wanted to tell her I loved her, but I knew that that would sound even more artificial and manipulative, though, again, I believed it was true. "I've never felt about a girl the way I feel about you, honest, and I've never touched anyone in that way before."

Gloria pulled back from me, letting the blanket fall from her shoulders. "Will," she said, her voice full of sadness. "I just can't do that—not yet, anyway. Can't we just let the evening end like this? I'm sorry."

"No, I'm sorry," I said, and I felt the aching passion subside in me as she held her face up beneath the distant streetlight and stared into my eyes.

"I'm not a tease, Will, honest. I'd never do that to you. It's just that I . . . I just can't do that." She looked away. "I'm sorry."

"Hey, it's okay. I understand," I said, though I didn't really understand at all. My physical longing for her was so great that I couldn't comprehend her not feeling exactly the same way, especially when she kissed me so passionately and breathlessly. But I wasn't going to risk ruining our friendship or even that single night. "We better go catch that bus," I said, sounding just a bit too cheerful.

"Will," she said again, not moving from where she stood. "Someday I'll explain all this to you. I'm just asking that you be patient with me. Okay?"

"Sure, I understand." I pulled the blanket from my shoulders, folded it and tucked it under my arm. I took her hand and began to walk toward the streetlight.

Thirteen

ON THE FOLLOWING SATURDAY, Tom called to find out if I could meet him after work. He said we needed to go out and celebrate, though he didn't say what the celebration was about. He worked at a gas station near his house and would be done with work shortly before my shift ended around ten. My father was out of town and my mother had always been doting to the point of negligence about any curfew. I told him I would meet him after work, though there was some desperate pressure to his voice that caused a faint stirring of nervousness in me.

Tom was already waiting for me when I exited the kitchen. He didn't speak until we had gotten into his car and he had started the engine. "I've got two six-packs of Stite on the floor in back," he said as he shifted the Ford into reverse.

"Two six-packs? What the hell is going on, Tom?"

"I told you we were going to celebrate."

"Hey, I don't know what the hell we're celebrating, but I can't get all skunked up on beer tonight."

Tom pulled out of the lot and took a left onto Lake Street. "Relax, we aren't drinking it alone. We're going to pick up the O'Hara twins."

I had never met Jean or Jan O'Hara, but I had heard about them. "The red-headed twins?"

"The same."

I thought immediately of Gloria. "Damn it, Tom. No, I'm not doing this."

Tom looked straight ahead and stomped on the gas as we headed toward the light on Cedar. "Hey, you aren't married to Gloria." he said, as if my thoughts had been spoken aloud. "You don't have to tell her every damned little thing that you do. You're my friend and I've asked you to celebrate with me tonight."

I knew I could never match Tom's anger or stubbornness. "Okay," I said as calmly as I could, "just what are we celebrating tonight?"

He turned and glanced at me. "You haven't heard?" he said, his voice full of legitimate surprise.

"Heard what?"

"Little Miss Sweetness found a new boyfriend. So, I figure I might as well go out and have some fun."

"Cindy? Cindy found a new boyfriend?" I hadn't talked to her or seen her at work recently. I had heard nothing about her dating someone new.

"Yeah, little Miss Proper found some prick at Roosevelt who was more her style."

"Man, I'm sorry, Tom. I had no idea."

Tom slammed on the brakes and screeched to a halt at a red light on Hiawatha Avenue. The car took a short-lived nosedive. Tom turned to me and winked as the car leveled again. "Hey, don't worry about it. It was never going to work out anyway. We were just too different to ever last." He forced a quick laugh and punched me on the arm. "Now the O'Hara twins—there's a couple of girls after my heart. I've always kind of liked Jan, but then Jean is probably just as good." I could see the muscles in his forearms flex and relax and flex again as he gripped the steering wheel.

"Tom . . ."

"You know what they say, the O'Hara twins aren't that easy—you have to ask for what you want."

Tom was facing the world as he had always faced it, denying pain and striking out in whatever manner was available to him. The only sin was the sin of weakness. "Tom, look, I don't think this is going to do anyone any—"

"God damn it, Will! Are you my friend or aren't you? I'm asking you to spend a couple of fucking hours with me. Okay?"

I had never seen Tom more intense or angrier. He was as raw and sensitive as an exposed nerve. I knew there was no reasoning with him at the moment, no logic that could prevail over his emotions. "All right, Tom. All right."

* * * * *

The O'Hara twins were waiting for us on a street corner and ran toward the car as we neared the curb. They were both dressed in shorts and sleeveless blouses, the colors indistinct in the dark. One of the twins had a ponytail while the other wore her hair in a flip. The twin with the flip reached my door first and leaned in to greet us. "Hi, Tom. Is this cute guy Will?" she said.

"Hi, Jan—or did you switch your hairdo again?" Tom asked.

The girl leaning in the window laughed. "No, I haven't switched my hairdo. Will, I'm Jan and this is my sister, Jean," she said as her twin neared the window.

"Hi, Jan and Jean," I said as I opened the door and started to get out of the car.

"Jan, you can sit up here with me and Jean and Will can get to know each other in the back seat," Tom directed.

"God, you're awful, Tom," Jan said as she and her sister followed Tom's instructions.

I held the door open for Jean and pulled the seat forward so she could get into the back. After she slid across the back seat, I got in and found that she immediately pulled close to me, so that our thighs were touching. "Nice to meet you, Will," she said and smiled.

Other than the hairdos, I really couldn't tell one girl from the other. Their voices were indistinguishable to me. They both had round, innocent looking faces with large, pale eyes—either blue or gray, I couldn't tell which in the night—and tiny noses that couldn't escape the descriptor of "button." "Yeah, it's nice to meet you too," I said.

Tom looked back over the seat before he pulled away from the curb. "We have Stite for everyone. I thought we'd take it over to Nokomis and see how the lake looks at night."

"All right," the twins sang out in unison and did a little bouncy dance in their seats.

Tom pulled away from the curb, made a U-turn at the corner and headed south toward Lake Nokomis, one hand on the steering wheel as the other rubbed Jan O'Hara's back.

"You and Tom are both baldies, right?" Jean said to me. Her reference was to the generally accepted division of local male teenagers into two essential categories: greasers and baldies. The greasers wore long hair, slicked with Brylcreem or some other hair tonic and combed into ducktails or DAs, and tended in their dress toward motorcycle jackets, blue jeans and boots. The baldies wore their hair short and typically dressed in button-down shirts, sweaters, khaki pants and dress shoes. Neither category constituted a true gang, but it seemed a useful reference for some people and there was, in fact, a vague and ill-defined tension between those who fell into one category or the other.

"Well, I don't have my membership card yet and I haven't been to any of the meetings."

"What?"

"Sorry," I said, realizing that she was only trying to be friendly and wasn't the real object of my anger. "Yeah, I guess you could call Tom and me baldies."

"That's okay," she said as she slipped her arm around mine and hugged my upper arm, her right breast pressed hard against my triceps. "I got nothing against baldies at all." She seemed so sincere about the generosity of her viewpoint that I nearly laughed.

"That's good." I said.

Within twenty minutes we were at Lake Nokomis, cruising slowly around the northern rim of the lake, somewhere between the main beach to the west and the little beach along the eastern shore. Tom killed the lights on the car and rolled silently to a stop. Across the road was a grassy area that ran maybe thirty yards toward the lake. There were several clusters of birch trees near the lakeshore. The water looked black as tar just beyond the trees. The night was warm and still and the water gave only the slightest twinkling, scattered reflections of moonlight.

"Hey, bust out that Stite," Tom said as he turned toward me.

I opened three cans and passed them around and then opened one for myself. Tom and Jan took their beer and before either of them had taken three swallows they slipped below the top of the seat and out of sight. I could hear Jan giggling and Tom saying something about her doing whatever she wanted to do. I had an urge to bolt from the car and run as fast and as far as I could.

"Is something bothering you?" Jean said.

"I'm just not . . . I really shouldn't be out here tonight," I said.

"You seem like a really nice guy. Is there something I can do to make you feel better?" As she spoke she ran a hand up and down my left thigh.

"Tell him to lighten up and enjoy himself," Tom boomed from the front seat and laughed. His head bobbed up for a moment and then disappeared again below the seat back. His hand came over the seat. "Give me another beer."

I stuck my beer in his hand, which instantly disappeared again below the seat. "Look, Jean, there's a girl I really like, and I don't feel right about being out here tonight."

"Yeah," she said, seemingly unfazed by my news, "are you going steady with her?"

"Well, not exactly."

"Well, hey, we're just having a few laughs. What's the harm?"

"You tell 'em, Jean," Tom's response from the front seat was immediate.

Jean stopped rubbing my leg and stared at me, searching my eyes and face until I was uncomfortable with her silence. "What?" I said at last.

"Let's get out of this car and go sit by the lake. Come on, come on," she said and began pulling on my arm. "Jan, open the damn door. Me and Will are going to go sit by the water. You and Tom can have the rest of the beer if you want."

"Let them out," Tom's voice sounded muffled and far away.

Jean pulled me by the hand as she ran across the street and onto the grassy area. She found a rocky ledge between two trees where we slipped off our shoes and dangled our feet in the water. She took a sip of her Stite and then turned toward me. "You want the rest of this?"

"No thanks."

She set the can down next to her on the flat stone. "Are you in love with this girl you mentioned?"

I was surprised by her question and began to find her directness and spontaneity amusing, even endearing, despite my regrets about being with her. And there was a sort of rough-edged sweetness about her that made some part of me inexplicably sad. "I think maybe I am."

"Yeah, no kidding? What's her name?"

"Gloria Jensen. Do you know her?"

"I don't know her, but I've heard of her." She kicked her feet back and forth alternately in the water, the little splashing sounds crisp and clear in the stillness of the night. "Yeah, what do you like about her so much?" She turned and squinted at me, as if she needed to watch my face to determine the veracity of my answer.

"Well, everything, I guess. She's honest and pretty and smart. I don't know. I just feel that the two of us are the same in some way. Maybe that sounds stupid."

"Yeah? Hmm. Most guys I know are pretty much interested in one thing when it comes to girls, you know?" She turned away from me and looked out at the lake. She stopped kicking her feet back and forth, leaned back, her arms straight and angled behind her, the palms of her hands resting on the rocky ledge. She raised her face up to the starry sky and closed her eyes. "I know what most people think of me and Jan, but we don't care." She kept her eyes closed and her head tilted back. She didn't speak for a long time, breathing the night air deeply. "Do you think I'm pretty?" she said at last. She asked the question flatly, without any hint of urgency or hope for praise.

"Yes, I think you're very pretty."

"Hmm." She sounded pleased, even happy with my answer. She sat motionless for a few moments and then turned to me again. She smiled broadly, "Let's go for a swim."

"What?"

Jean stood and began to unbutton her blouse. "Come on. Let's go for a swim." She threw her blouse on the grass and pulled me by the hand. "Come on, it's a perfect night for skinny-dipping." She let go of my hand and pulled down her shorts and threw them beside her blouse. She stood over me, now dressed only in her panties and bra, her legs spread wide. "Come on, Will. It's a perfect night. Let's not waste it."

"Jean, get your clothes back on. What the hell are you doing?"

She laughed and turned toward the water. "I'm going for a swim. You can come with me or you can sit on the shore and watch. Eeeeeowww," she shouted as she plowed through the water until it was up to her waist. She turned and looked back at me, her arms now crossed, her fists tucked up under her chin. "Come on, Will. Don't be a chicken."

"Jean, get out of there. Come on."

She stopped moving and didn't speak, letting the little eddies of her own wake lap against her waist and slap her now outstretched hands. Her body was as white as ivory against the lake, her features indistinct, but even in the darkness I could see that she was looking beyond me now, staring past me toward the street and Tom's car. "Shit, Will, is that the cops?"

I turned to look back at where Tom's car was parked. Approaching from the rear of the car was a squad. The black-and-white had its spotlight on and was sweeping it back and forth along the shoreline. Still out of the spotlight's range, I rolled my pant legs up as far as I could and ran into the water toward Jean. "Get over here, Jean." I motioned her toward me, grabbed her hand and pulled her down near the shoreline where we were partially hidden by the trees. My heart was racing as I watched the squad approach a car parked ten or fifteen yards behind Tom's. I could hear Jean giggling and feel her brush herself against my arm.

"Hey, I finally got you in the water. You're going to get all wet. Why don't you take your pants off?" She laughed and slipped backward, but kept her grip on my arm.

"Damn it, Jean, it isn't funny. Just stay down and be quiet."

I watched as both cops got out of the squad and approached the car parked behind Tom's. One cop stood at the driver's window while the other one walked slowly to the back of the car. The light atop the squad was on and rotating, bathing Tom's car in a beam of red light over and over again. While the cops remained occupied with the first car, I saw the lights on Tom's car come on and watched as he slowly pulled away from the curb.

"Hey," Jean shouted, "your buddy is leaving us."

"Shhh! Don't worry about Tom, as soon as he can, he'll be back for us."

"Yeah? Well, then I'm gonna have the rest of my can of Stite while we wait for him," Jean said.

She let go of my arm and began walking unsteadily toward the spot where we had been sitting. She seemed intent on recovering her beer or possibly on revealing our presence to the police, I couldn't tell which. "Jean, get the hell back here. Jean!"

She stopped midway between the trees and where the beer sat on shore, clearly within sight from the road. "All right. Don't have a kitten." She started back toward me. "You baldies aren't really all that much fun."

When she was close enough, I grabbed her hand and pulled her to me. In my rush to make sure she was out of sight, I pulled too hard and caused us both to tumble backward into the water, drenching myself from the waist down. This caused a fit of laughter from Jean that I was sure could be heard across the entire lake.

"You . . . you . . . ha . . . you should have . . . you should have taken your clothes off. Oh, oh, my God." She was breathless with laughter. "Ha. You should have taken your clothes off. See . . . ha . . . see."

I stood and pulled her closer to me as I edged our way to the trees. I could feel the water running out of my rolled-up pants and down my legs. I began to laugh myself and at the same time continued to try and quiet her down. "Stop it . . . ha . . . oh, shit . . . ha . . . stop it."

We ducked down amid the clump of trees and watched the squad slowly restart its patrol along the road, its spotlight again sweeping back and forth along the shoreline. In less than five minutes, I saw Tom's car pull up and park in the approximate spot he had left earlier. Jean and I emerged from the water, still laughing as she put on her clothes and finished her can of Stite.

Fourteen

Tom didn't tell me anything more about his breakup with Cindy. He only repeated that she had found someone else and they were done with each other. Maybe that was all there was to know, but I didn't find his attempted display of indifference about what had happened believable. When he picked me up at the restaurant on nights he knew she would be working, he waited in the lot for me. And when Cindy and I worked the same shift, she didn't speak at all about Tom and acted as though nothing had ever happened between them. Their behavior struck me as odd and secretive, but it was, I reasoned, their concern and not mine. And so my questions about whatever facts were behind the matter simply faded away. We didn't see the O'Hara twins again, and when I talked about telling Gloria what had happened Tom gave me a lecture on "growing up." He shook his head, as though I were some intractable child whose thinking was not clear or sophisticated enough to understand the situation.

"Not a damn thing happened," he said. "All you're going to do by telling her about it is piss her off. Just leave it the hell alone. What she doesn't know won't hurt her." His advice seemed ultimately practical, and yet there was an element of dishonesty about all of it that bothered me.

"Wouldn't the nuns have called that a sin of omission?" I said, only partially joking.

"Shit," Tom said, and that was his final comment on the subject.

The days of summer slipped by quickly. We didn't take our promised trip north, as Dee needed to keep working in order to pay her fall tuition and I really preferred to stay home where I could continue to see Gloria and put in as many hours as possible at the restaurant and save for a car. And that didn't go as well as I had hoped—saving for a car. I was able to pass the test for my driver's license and I had purchased clothes for school that were more stylish than what I had worn the previous year, but setting money aside for a car had been nearly impossible. I thought I could probably buy a decent used car for around two hundred dollars and that I would have that amount set aside before the summer was over. But with what I spent on clothing, occasional dates with Gloria, and money placed in a savings account at my mother's insistence, it became clear that I would have less than one hundred dollars by the time school started. The realization of my daydreams would be delayed. My dream of driving with Gloria beside me, nestling close, the two of us going off on a date alone, needed to wait a little longer.

For weeks I had been thinking about not trying out for football in my junior year, knowing Jim would want me to work more hours at the restaurant than football practice would allow, and also realizing that my chances for making the varsity team were not all that great. And while I had enjoyed playing on the sophomore squad, some of the vaunted school spirit of it had been lost for me after what had happened between Sonny Holmes and Leo Stevens. My real dreams and priorities required money—money I couldn't make if I was playing ball. Tom planned to play again, and to my surprise didn't lobby me too hard about playing a second year. He said he understood why I wanted to make as much money as possible during the school year and that he probably would do the same thing, were he in my situation. He said if his choice was a car or football, he'd give up football too.

The first day of junior year, no doubt to someone's great personal satisfaction, started with a literal bang. During homeroom we were advised that a firecracker had exploded that morning in the administrative office and the principal would appreciate any information regarding the person or persons involved in this senseless prank. While we weren't able to hear the explosion from our vantage point in room 112, I think everyone appreciated being advised that it had happened—at least that appeared to be the case, judging from the snickering of the students. I couldn't be sure, but

I thought I caught a slight grin on Mrs. Swanson's face as she read her notes.

As Mrs. Swanson continued with the opening day announcements, I felt Ray Sanders tap me on the shoulder. Arranged in alphabetical order by surname, Ray sat directly behind me. "Hey, man, look at this," Ray whispered.

"What?"

"Look at this, Ross."

I turned slightly, and tried to keep my eyes on Mrs. Swanson and take just a second to steal a glance at whatever it was that Ray wanted me to see. I looked down quickly to see the back of Ray's right hand with a Band-Aid running from one side to the other. Ray was black and the back of his hand was as dark as a coffee bean. The Band-Aid was a sort of pale orange hue and the contrast of skin and bandage was striking. "What happened?"

"Nothing, man, but I'm pissed."

"Why?"

"The box said 'flesh colored' Band-Aids. Does that look flesh colored to you?"

"You've got to be kidding."

He barely suppressed a laugh. "No, man, look at it. It doesn't match at all, and the box said the Band-Aids were flesh colored."

I turned back toward the front of the room to see if we were attracting Mrs. Swanson's attention. She seemed unaware of our conversation as she continued on with morning announcements. I leaned my head back slightly and whispered out of the side of my mouth, "They should probably offer some kind of variety pack, you know. I mean, I'm not orange, either. I'm not sure who that would match."

This caused Ray to laugh out loud and slap me on the back. Mrs. Swanson looked up from her announcements. "Raymond, do you and Will have something you'd like to share with the rest of the class?"

"No, Mrs. Swanson," Ray said.

"Will, is there something you want to tell all of us?"

"No, Mrs. Swanson. I'm sorry."

When the announcements were done and the warning bell rang, Ray tapped me on the shoulder again. "Hey, man, how come you aren't out for football this year?"

"I'm working and want to put enough money together to get a car, so I really don't have the time. Besides, let's face it, I wasn't going to make varsity, anyway."

Ray nodded. I wasn't sure if it was a nod of understanding or agreement that I was never going to play varsity, or both. "Well, the coach was badmouthing you at practice yesterday. I think if it was up to him you'd get a yellow Band-Aid. He kept talking about quitters and how he doesn't have time for them. It was some bad shit."

"Really?"

"I wouldn't shit you, man."

I could feel my face flush as both anger and embarrassment at being ridiculed in front of the football team welled up in me. "He called me a quitter? What the hell, it isn't like I'm some star who's hurting the team by leaving."

Ray gathered up his books and stood as the second bell rang. "He didn't use your name, but everyone knew who he was talking about—or at least all the junior players knew."

I fell in step behind Ray as we headed for the door. "How do you feel about me not trying out for the team?'

Ray looked back and smiled. "That's your business, man. Besides, it's just one less guy I have to worry about." Ray slapped me on the back and turned to head in the opposite direction as we exited the room.

As I walked down the crowded hallway I spotted Coach Phillips coming toward me, his head rising above most of the students. When we were less than twenty feet apart, I caught his eye. He quickly turned away, looked to his left and went down an adjoining hallway. There was no doubt in my mind that he had purposely avoided me or, more accurately, had shunned me. The mixture of anger and hurt caused my throat to knot up. I could feel my face grow hot with embarrassment once again.

My first hour class was English. Junior Kandowski was one of the first people I spotted when I entered the room. He was already seated, his text open, his long legs stretched out into the aisle. I approached him immediately, though my emotions were still in riot and I was barely able to put my thoughts together. "Junior," I croaked.

Junior looked up and smiled his big, broad smile. "Hey, Will. Good to see you. Did you have a good summer?"

"Yeah, good to see you, too. I was working most of the summer." I knew I was rushing and probably sounded strange, even rude, but I wanted to get to my questions before class began. "Hey, Junior, you're out for football again this year, right?"

"Right."

"I was just talking to Ray Sanders and he told me Coach Phillips was putting me down for not coming out for the team this year. And then I just saw the coach in the hall and he acted like I had the plague or something. I don't get it. What's so terrible about me not playing football?"

The smile faded from Junior's face. He pulled his legs up under his desk and leaned forward. "The coach did talk about not wanting anyone else to quit the team, and he got sort of carried away, but he never mentioned your name."

"But everyone knew it was me he was talking about, right?"

"I don't know, maybe. But I don't think you're the only one who played last year and didn't come back out again this year."

"Damn it, Junior, I think he's being unfair as hell. I need to work and I probably wasn't ever going to play that much anyway. It's not like I'm some big star who's screwing the team over by not playing."

Junior considered for a moment. When he spoke again he picked his words carefully, as if the most important thing in the world at that moment was my understanding of what had happened. "There isn't one guy on that team who's mad at you or thinks you've done anything wrong. I'm sure of that. As for the coach, you have to remember that he makes his living coaching football, so he probably hates losing anyone's interest. It's his job."

Junior could probably see the tension leave my body as he spoke those words. "Well, I still think he's a jerk for running the other way when he saw me in the hall."

"Yeah, that sounds pretty bad. I'll give you that." Then a heartbeat later, he said, "Maybe he thought over what he said and now he's embarrassed about it." Junior chuckled and the broad smile returned to his face.

"Yeah, maybe," I said.

"Everyone please take a seat. Please, everyone take a seat," Mrs. Bridges called out over the din of students. "You may sit wherever you want, but please sit."

I found an open desk two back from Junior. I sat down, feeling much better than I had just a few minutes earlier in the hall. I exhaled. I felt as if I had been holding my breath from the time Ray Sanders had talked to me until I had had the chance to speak with Junior.

Mrs. Bridges stood before the class cradling a clipboard in her right arm. "Welcome to junior English. If you are not here for junior English, you are in the wrong room. I am Mrs. Bridges and I'll be taking attendance in a minute or two. As our very first order of business, I want you all to know that we are going to begin this class by studying the romantic English poets of the eighteenth century."

The entire class moaned as if on cue.

Mrs. Bridges, gray-haired and cadaverously thin, with a tight-lipped smile that somehow made us feel as if we were her secret allies, paused and looked out over her glasses at the class. "Well done. I fully expected that, but I promise you that you will all be pleasantly surprised. In this class you will discover things about yourself and about poetry and literature that you never expected." She winked at us. "I promise."

Fifteen

Neither Gloria nor Tom was in any of my classes. That was disappointing, but probably helped me in terms of my ability to concentrate in school. Despite getting Junior's positive take on my having quit the football team, I was troubled enough by what I had heard to ask Tom about it too. Tom was just as reassuring as Junior, though in a much different style. "Who cares what Coach Phillips thinks?" he said. "He's got a football for a brain."

I continued to work twenty hours a week, sometimes more with extended weekend hours, and with school now underway there were only rare opportunities to see Gloria. She was working too, and our schedules usually didn't mesh well. We talked on the phone when we could, and finally there was another one of those weeknight evenings when she and I could spend some time at her house. Ironically, this time we were really going to try and help each other with a school assignment, even though we were in separate classes. We were both struggling with Mrs. Bridges's English poets—though admittedly Gloria was struggling less than I was—and thought we could go over some of the poems together. That, and the fact that her parents might come home at any time, kept us away from the TV and the couch in the living room. We were also discussing the possibility of going to the homecoming game and dance. Achieving that seemed as vexing as understanding the poetry.

Tom wasn't going to the dance, so there was no chance of doubling with him, and there really wasn't anyone else I felt comfortable asking about a possible double date. Gloria's girlfriends either weren't going to homecoming or were already doubling with some other couple. I still had no car and the chance of borrowing my father's car was so slight as to be rejected as a realistic possibility. Gloria sat across from me at her kitchen table, her head hung low over her textbook. She had grown silent and pushed her hair back behind her ears distractedly. After a moment, she slid the textbook away and looked up at me and smiled. "You know, it really isn't that important to me that we go to homecoming."

"Really?" I could feel Josephine rubbing herself against my legs, purring as she continued to weave back and forth between my ankles.

"Really. I mean, I'd have to spend money on a dress and we'd both miss hours at work. I don't know, it just seems like so much bother for one night."

She didn't say anything about my not having a car, which eased my feelings of guilt and insecurity. "Are you really sure about not going, Gloria? I know it's kind of a big deal."

She looked directly in my eyes and smiled at me and my passion for her at the moment was so great that I had to look away. "Let's agree that we'll go next year, when we're both seniors. How about that, Mr. Ross?"

I looked at her again. "Yes. We can plan ahead for it, and I know I'll have my own car by then. You're my date for next year. No backing out on this," I said.

"No backing out." She reached out and pulled the text back and opened it to the poem we had been reading. It was "Ode: Intimations of Immortality from Recollections of Early Childhood" by William Wordsworth. "Listen to the last two lines of the poem," she said, and then read them to me. "To me the meanest flower that blows can give thoughts that do often lie too deep for tears."

"Yeah, I mean, who talks like that?" I joked. I felt lighter now that we had agreed on what to do about homecoming—and happy that she saw us still together next year. I could feel Josephine again beneath the table.

"Seriously, Will, I think Wordsworth is saying that the smallest things in life can be the most important—or at least, that we can find the greatest pleasure and deepest meaning in them." She closed the book and looked up at me. "When I was small and my mom would talk about my dad, it was always little things that she talked about—how he called her his angel, how he could always find a way to make her laugh when she was angry or sad. It was all those little memories that seemed most important to her." The hint of a smile on her face faded as she closed the book and slid it away. She stood and stretched. "Would you like some more Coke or something?"

"No, I'm fine."

She picked up her glass and went to the refrigerator and got another Coke. "I don't think my mom will ever get over losing him," she said as she sat back down at the table. She took a swallow of her drink. "I think she sees life and men a lot differently since she made the mistake of marrying Martin."

"Really?" I said nothing more, sensing that it was best to let her talk without distracting her or chasing her off topic with my usual interruptions.

Gloria held her glass at arm's length and cupped it in both hands. She turned the glass round and round on the tabletop and was silent for a long time. "Martin is a true rat. I think Mom knows it but won't ever admit it to herself."

"A rat?"

"Yeah," she said as she stared at her glass of Coke and continued to turn it around. "He doesn't know it, but I saw him out with another woman once. I never told my mom, and I never will, but I think down deep she knows he's a rat too."

"Maybe you made a mistake—about what you saw."

Gloria looked up at me and stopped twirling her glass. She let out a brief puff of breath between her pursed lips that conveyed her certainty about what she had seen. "I didn't make a mistake. It was two years ago. I was coming back from the store and I saw him in his car with another woman. When he stopped at a light she started kissing him. He didn't see me, but they weren't more than thirty feet away from me."

"And you never said anything to your mom?"

Gloria began to twirl her glass again. "I wanted to tell her, but I just couldn't. She's been hurt enough. I just couldn't be the one to tell her about it and see her hurt all over again."

"Oh, Gloria, I'm really sorry."

"Yeah, I wish she'd never married him—I think she wishes the same thing sometimes."

"I'm sorry," I repeated. "Maybe it was something he did that won't happen again. I mean, maybe it was some stupid one time fling or something."

"Yeah, maybe," she said, with no conviction. "Well, I know one thing for sure." She looked at me and set her jaw in a fiercely determined look I had never seen on her before. "That isn't going to be my life. I'll never make the mistake of marrying someone who can't be trusted, or because I'm lonely and afraid."

"No," I said and felt some vague and fleeting sense of guilt that I didn't understand.

"I'll tell you something else about him—" she began, but the back door opened and interrupted her. Bags of groceries filled the doorway. "Gloria," a man's voice called out from behind the brown bags. "Give your mother and me a hand with these, will you?"

I stood up and backed away from the table. Martin Scully and Gloria's mother entered the kitchen, both with their arms full of overflowing brown paper bags. Gloria got up from the table too and we both went to help with the groceries. Gloria took a bag from her mother as I approached Mr. Scully. "I'd be happy to give you a hand with those, Mr. Scully," I said as I approached.

The bags lowered and a dark-haired man about my size with heavy, black eyebrows that rose in an arc of surprise appeared from behind the bags. He was clean-shaven, but his beard was so heavy that it looked gray-blue in the kitchen light. His jaw was slack with evident surprise as he handed one of the bags to me. "And who are you?" he asked as I placed the bag on the table.

I took the second bag from him and then turned back and held out my hand. "I'm Will Ross, Mr. Scully. I'm a friend of Gloria's from school."

Mr. Scully stared at me and made no attempt to shake my outstretched hand. "Yeah?" He turned to Gloria's mother. "I'll go out and get the rest of the groceries. You can start putting these away," he said, and with that he headed for the back door.

"Martin . . ." Gloria's mother called after him, but he continued out the door without looking back. She turned to me and held out her hand. "You'll have to excuse my husband. He's had a tough day."

"All his days are tough," Gloria mumbled, so that only I could hear her.

"I'm Mrs. Scully, Gloria's mother. It is so nice to finally meet you, Will. Gloria's told us so much about you. She mentioned that you would be stopping over today, I think Martin maybe just forgot."

"It's nice to meet you too, Mrs. Scully." She held out her hand and I clasped it gently in both of mine. She smiled at me and I was struck by how much Gloria resembled her mother, except for the eyes. Her mother's eyes were a much lighter shade of brown than Gloria's and there was a look of sadness about them that went beyond the delicate wrinkles that appeared at the corners as she smiled. There was an indefinable weariness about her she could not mask. "Gloria and I were going over a poetry assignment. We're about done now, so I'll be leaving in a minute."

"There's no need for you to rush off, Will. Why don't you stay for a while and we can talk. We could all sit down and have a Coke or coffee and talk."

At that moment Martin banged into the kitchen with his arms full of additional grocery bags. "Come on, come on, let's get this stuff put away, people," he said as he shoved the new bags onto the table.

Gloria's mother began plucking canned goods from the bags and opening and closing cupboard doors as she put them away. Gloria moved at a somewhat more leisurely pace with items for the refrigerator. As I watched the two of them following Martin's commands, I felt a sense of loathing for the man. "Well, I've really got to be getting back home," I said to the three of them. "It was nice meeting you, Mrs. Scully."

Gloria's mom looked back over her shoulder from where she stood at the cupboard. "It was nice meeting you too, Will. You'll have to come back soon and visit." Martin Scully said nothing as he stood and stared at me.

"I'll do that," I said. And then I decided that I wasn't going to leave like some timorous, inconsequential being who withered under Martin Scully's stare. "It was nice meeting you too, sir," I said in the most stentorian voice I could muster as I again extended my hand toward him. I continued to hold my hand out, not allowing him to ignore me. He waited a moment but finally reached out and shook my hand.

"Yeah, nice to meet you too," he mumbled.

"I'll walk you to the door, Will," Gloria said as she turned away from the refrigerator.

The two of us left the kitchen and headed for the front door, followed close behind by Josephine. I turned and took Gloria's hands and squeezed them just before we reached the front door. I leaned toward her and whispered, "You're right, he seems like a real dink. What else were you going to tell me about him?"

"I'll explain another time," she whispered, and then she smiled and squeezed my hands in return. "See ya, Will," she said and gave me a conspiratorial wink.

Sixteen

In late September, Bea hired a new boy to work the counter and fountain at the Shadow Box. His name was Bill Freeman. I knew him slightly from school. Bill was tall and gangly and wore thick glasses that made his eyes look as though they might, at any moment, bulge out of their sockets. He was one of those kids who was a magnet for taunting by other students and more than once had been on the losing end of a calculated and hostile encounter in gym class. Despite the episodes of meanness that punctuated his life, he was unfailingly pleasant and wore a perpetual smile that seemed to irritate Jim. In fact, it quickly became apparent that almost anything he did irritated Jim. And predictably, Jim was not given to patiently instructing him regarding his serving errors or above humiliating him in front of the staff. This became evident on the second day of Bill's employment when he came to the window of the kitchen and called out an order for one of his counter customers.

"One beef plate, please," Bill said, as he bent down to look in the kitchen window.

Jim slammed a metal serving spoon on the shelf of the steam table. "What the hell does that mean? Do you want a hot beef sandwich, a beef dinner or a cold beef sandwich? Don't come back here and holler out an order and not know what the hell you're talking about." Jim turned and looked at me and scowled, as if seeking some sort of confirmation regarding Bill's unbelievable ineptness.

I looked away from Jim and glanced up at Bill. His cheeks were red and his eyes bulged beyond their normally extreme limits. He mumbled an apology and left for the counter, apparently to get necessary clarification from the customer. In a moment he returned and called out, "One hot beef sandwich, please."

Jim glared at him. "Now is that a new order or is it the order you screwed up just a minute ago?"

Several waitresses turned to look at Bill. His face grew even more flushed and for an instant I thought he might cry. "That's the order I messed up a minute ago."

Jim continued to glare at Bill and began putting the sandwich together at the steam table. When the hot beef sandwich was ready, Jim tossed the plate up onto the counter and I saw a dollop of gravy splash onto Bill's white serving jacket. I thought it was all incredibly unfair of Jim to treat him as he did. After all, I thought, he was a novice, just finding his way, and Jim's intolerance for any perceived error simply made Bill all the more nervous and prone to making more mistakes. I said nothing, however, fearing that I would then become an additional target of Jim's wrath.

Bill managed to avoid any further humiliation from Jim for the next several days, even working through the Sunday morning breakfast rush without incident. In the afternoon, while Jim was in the basement taking his usual mid-day rest, business dropped off to a near standstill. During the lull, Bill left the counter to be watched by one of the waitresses while he came back to the kitchen to see me. He poked his head through the doorway to the kitchen at the far end of the steam table. "Hey, Will, is Jim taking his nap?" he said in an excited whisper.

"Yeah, he went downstairs about twenty minutes ago. Why?"

He looked back and forth across the length of the kitchen, as if my statement should still be taken with all due caution.

"How long will he be down there?"

"Probably another hour, I guess. Why? What's up?"

A grin spread across Bill's face and he stepped into the kitchen. "I got something I want to show you, if you've got a second. This is a riot."

"Yeah, what's a riot?"

He stared at me through his thick glasses, the corners of his eyes wrinkled with child-like delight. "Have you ever heard of blue blazers?" While he waited for my answer, he couldn't withhold a coarse burst of laughter.

"I don't think so. What are they?"

Bill was still laughing and not able to answer immediately. "If you hold a match near your butt when you fart, you get this blue flame. They call them blue blazers."

"Get out of here," I said, "you're making that up."

Bill laughed again. "No, no, I'm not kidding you. It really works. I didn't believe it at first either, but it's true."

It was then that I noticed he had come prepared with a book of matches. And I could only assume that he was also in a state of flatulent readiness. I looked out into the dining room. I couldn't see any customers, and most of the waitresses were standing around the silverware stations talking to each other. "Okay," I said, "I'm calling you on this. Come back by the break table in the corner. I've got to see this."

"Okay," he said, as we headed to the corner of the kitchen. There was a butcher-block table and two chairs where the cooks could take their meal and cigarette breaks. "Just sit over there and check this out."

I sat down while Bill, standing a respectable distance from me, turned his back toward me and struck a match. "Ready?" he said, and bent forward and looked back toward his buttocks. He held the match not more than an inch away from the seat of his pants. I heard a slight grunt from Bill, which was followed by the staccato sounds of flatus and a burst of blue flame that flared the length of the seam in the back of his slacks. "Did you see that?" he said.

"Holy shit, did I ever see it." I said, and then the two of us began to laugh hysterically. I kept laughing until my stomach began to ache and a film of tears came to my eyes.

"You want to try it?" Bill asked, as he held out the matches.

I waved him away. "I can't," I managed to get out as I laughed. "I don't need to fart right now," I said, and then began to laugh even harder at my own statement.

Bill recovered a degree of sobriety and looked around the kitchen. "Hey, I gotta go, but I'll be back in a few minutes," he said and headed out of the kitchen to the fountain. I wiped tears from my eyes and walked back beyond the steam table to the grills.

There were no orders on the counter and I could see that the waitresses were still busy visiting at the silverware stations or putting dinner inserts in the menus.

After a few minutes, Bill returned to the kitchen. "Hey, Will, I think I've got a rip-snorter this time."

The two of us headed back to the break table and I again took my seat to watch another fascinating display of his human pyrotechnics. "Okay," I said, "let's see what you've got."

Bill positioned himself as he had earlier. "Ready?"

The instant he struck the match, I saw Jim coming up the basement steps, his head rising above the kitchen floor just beyond Bill. I waved my arms wildly, trying to signal Bill to abort his demonstration, but it was too late. Just as Jim looked up into the kitchen area, there was an explosive sound from Bill and a blue flash even larger than the one I had seen earlier. There was a roar of laughter from Bill, followed by Jim's angry, booming voice.

"What in the hell is going on up here?"

Bill's laughter stopped immediately as he straightened up and faced Jim. From behind, I could see his neck grow pink and could only imagine the crimson color of his face. "I . . . I'm sorry. I . . . I was just . . ." Bill mumbled as he attempted to slip around Jim in a wide path and head back out to the counter.

Jim glared at Bill as he tried to circle around him. In his humiliation and shame, Bill appeared to me as though he was physically shrinking under Jim's gaze. "What the hell is the matter with you," Jim snarled as Bill passed him. "You ought to have your goddamned head examined, you know that? Now, get out of this kitchen and stay out." He continued to watch Bill until he had left the kitchen and was out of sight. He stood in the same spot without speaking. I was uncertain if I should move or say anything at all. Finally, he turned to me. "Is the steam table set up?"

"Yes."

"Then get over there and watch for orders,"

It was as gruff as he had ever spoken to me, but I considered myself lucky to not have gotten the same sort of treatment as Bill. I left the break table and walked back to the grill area.

Jim stayed at the break table and smoked cigarettes as I put up the few orders that began to trickle in as the afternoon wore on. Only Shirley, who was working the counter with Bill, brought any orders from the fountain area. I assumed Bill was avoiding any trips back to the kitchen, which I certainly understood. And as Jim sat in the corner of the kitchen brooding, I wasn't too sure that I was beyond paying some price for my involvement in the blue blazer fiasco. When he did finally join me near the steam table, he was silent and didn't look at me, which I took as a sign that he was still filled with anger but straining to keep from losing control and expressing it.

I picked up an order and handed it to him. "A dinner order, Jim."

He snatched the slip from me and began to dish up the order. After he placed the plate on the counter, he stared straight ahead while he spoke. "I'm going to have to talk to Bea about that kid. I just don't think he's going to work out here."

I knew if Jim told his wife that Bill needed to be let go, Bill's fate was sealed. I felt a wave of nervousness in my stomach, but said nothing. After a few moments of the two of us not looking at each other, Matt Patrick shuffled into the kitchen, tying his apron as he approached.

"The rush hasn't started yet, Matt," Jim said. "You can help Will with the short order stuff. I'll handle the steam table by myself."

I got the sense that Jim was still so angry he couldn't even tolerate anyone working in his proximity. Matt walked over to the sandwich table and stood beside me. "I don't have anything going right now, Matt," I told him. "It's been pretty slow so far."

Jim began to pace behind the steam table, as if he were a caged animal with only the length of the table in which to vent his energy. As he walked back and forth he shook his head, like a man recalling an incomprehensible incident. When he finally stopped pacing, he faced Matt and me. "I'm going to go talk to Bea for a little bit. Matt, you come over here and take care of the dinner orders. Will can handle any of the short order stuff by himself." With that he took off his apron and headed for the door and the dining room area.

Before Jim reached the door, I called out to him. "Jim," I said. It came out more loudly than I intended.

Jim spun around. "What?"

"Please don't," was all I could get out.

"Don't what?"

He glared at me, and I felt what I had said had only served to heighten his anger. "Please wait," I said. I left Matt and approached Jim, in the hope that keeping the matter more private would help to calm things. I lowered my voice. I didn't know how I was going to say it, but the words began to spill out before I could even give them any thought or order. "He didn't do anything worse than I did. We both knew it was stupid, but he's really a good guy and he puts up with so much crap from kids at school. This job means everything to him and I know he won't ever do anything like that again. If he loses his job his parents will kill him. I mean, he knows he bugs people, but he's trying so hard to do better." When I stopped to take a breath, I wasn't even sure of what I had said or if any of it had made any sense.

Jim stood and stared at me, his lips a thin, tight line of anger. He didn't speak for so long that I thought I might need to renew my plea, perhaps this time with a more thoughtful and articulate appeal. And then he spoke. "You tell that buddy of yours that if he ever pulls another stupid stunt like that, he'll be out the door and feel my boot on his ass for a week. I will not have those kinds of shenanigans going on in this kitchen—or anywhere else in this restaurant. Do you understand?"

"Yes." I couldn't believe what I had just heard. "So, he can stay? You aren't going to fire him?"

"Ah, what the hell good would it do me? The next kid Bea hired would probably be worse than this one." The tight line of his lips gave just the slightest hint of turning upward at the edges.

"Thanks, Jim. Thanks so much."

"Yeah, yeah. Get back over there and give Matt a hand, I have to talk to Bea about changing one of the items on the dinner menu."

* * * * *

Bill and I had worked the same shift and as we changed into our street clothes later that evening, I told him that Jim had been really angry with both of us but was letting it go this time. "We can't ever do something like that again."

"It won't ever happen again, but I get the feeling the guy really hates me, Will."

"He doesn't hate you at all. He's just tough on everyone when they first start. As a matter of fact, he told me he didn't want to let you go because they probably couldn't find anyone better than you."

Bill's eyes grew large behind his thick lenses, an incredulous look on his face. "Are you kidding me?"

"No. Honest to God, that's what he said. I mean the words aren't exact, but that's what he meant."

"That's great, Will. Thanks." He grinned as he slipped on his jacket.

Seventeen

I was glad Bill was able to keep his job, and felt good that I had spoken up before Jim had made an irreversible decision. In the days that followed, Bill began to venture back to the kitchen again to place his own orders for the counter customers. On the following Sunday, despite a couple of minor errors by Bill, there was no display of anger from Jim and no public humiliation of Bill. I felt a bit tense when Bill came back to place an order, and there were moments when I sensed Jim was biting down hard and holding his breath, but little by little the tension dissipated as the days and hours passed. And whenever I encountered Bill in the halls at school he would flash a big grin and call out to me and ask if I was working that night, though I knew he was aware of my schedule. It struck me how little it had taken to bring such an evident feeling of well-being to him. I couldn't help smiling back as I answered him, and in some small way feel that I had done something that was just a bit Junior-esque.

My good fortune continued with news from Tom during a mid-week lunch hour while he and I sat in Lida's Café as the jukebox thumped out a Bill Haley tune. One of the customers of the gas station where he worked had a car for sale. Tom said he wanted two-hundred-twenty-five dollars for the car, but was certain I could get it for two hundred. "It's a '49 Dodge Coronet, kind of a dark green with good tires—white sidewalls. It's a four-door but it's clean as hell and I know he's taken good care of it. It's got quite a bit of mileage on it, but it hardly burns any oil," he said as he took a long drag on his cigarette.

I really didn't know precisely what that meant, but I understood it was an endorsement of the car. The prospect of finally having my own car was exciting beyond description. "Well, I'll have the two hundred within a week. Do you think it'll sell before then?"

"I'll talk to him and tell him I have a friend who's interested in the car. He's a good guy. I think he'll give you a shot at it."

I was already envisioning Gloria sitting beside me as we drove away from her house, just the two of us, on a real date. "I'll have to have my dad take a look at it. He isn't too crazy about me driving and he'll want to see it," I said as reality seeped back into my consciousness.

"Sure. Anytime you can make it over to the station. Just let me know." Then he grinned. "I suppose your old man is worried about you drag racing up and down Lake Street just like James Dean in *Rebel Without A Cause*," he said, referring to a movie we'd seen together when we were just thirteen. We had both been so impressed by the teenage hero of the film that we had saved our paper route money to buy red windbreakers like the one James Dean had worn in the film.

"Sure," I said, "I'll be Jim Stark racing Buzz to Lake Calhoun."

Tom took another drag on his cigarette and squinted his eyes as he watched my face. "Yeah, it would be a nice car for dating Gloria. You're still seeing her, right?"

"When I can."

"Yeah. She's all right." A hint of a smile creased his face as he looked into the distance. His smile quickly faded. "I've been thinking of asking Jan O'Hara out again."

"Really?"

"Yeah, really," he said. "There's nothing wrong with Jan—or Jean for that matter."

"No. No, there's nothing wrong with them. I just thought you thought they were just . . . you know."

"Just what?"

"Just out for a good time and nothing more."

"Yeah, and what's wrong with that, Will?" He spoke the words as if they were a challenge. He took another long drag on his cigarette and exhaled out his mouth and nose simultaneously.

"Nothing, if that's all you care about."

"You know what, Will, the truth is that everyone's just out for a good time, they just go after it in different ways. I think the only thing that makes the O'Hara twins different from anyone else is that they happen to be more honest about what they want."

"All right, Tom," I said. "I have nothing against the O'Haras. Okay? I just guess I'm looking for something a little different in a girl than you are. And I think it's all more complicated than you say."

Tom took another drag and flicked the ash off his cigarette. He leaned back until his head touched the back of the high wooden booth. He exhaled a long stream of smoke and laughed. "Yeah, I guess that's what makes us different, Will. I don't think it's complicated at all."

* * * * *

I wasn't able to see or talk with Gloria until the next morning after homeroom. I was on my way to Mrs. Bridges's English class when I spotted Gloria on her way to first hour. I caught up with her and explained breathlessly that I might have a car within a week or so. I told her Tom had spotted it for me and that my father had agreed to help me check it out. She seemed almost as excited as I was. "That's great, Will. I hope you can get the car. I know how important it is to you."

"You get the first ride," I said as the warning bell rang. I turned and sprinted down the hall to my English class.

I entered the door just as the second bell rang. Mrs. Bridges peered out over her glasses at me and smiled as I slid into my seat. We were to discuss the poem "The Tyger" by the English poet, William Blake. I had read the poem but hadn't been able to study with Gloria or discuss it with anyone, and found it more than a little confusing and bewilderingly abstract. Mrs. Bridges began the discussion immediately, asking why we thought Blake had spelled "tiger" with a "y", and why he had talked about the tyger being in a forest rather than a jungle. My thoughts raced wildly between the hope that I wouldn't be called on, my dreams of the yet unseen 1949 Dodge Coronet, and Gloria.

"Please don't be afraid to say what you think the poem is about. Remember, much of the fun of literature is that it is open to interpretation. There aren't necessarily any right or wrong answers," Mrs. Bridges said as she began to walk down one aisle of desks and up another. "I want you to also consider the time period in which the poem was written and how that may have influenced William Blake." She stopped at my desk. I stared at the open text in front of me, wishing I could somehow disappear from her field of vision. When she called on one of the other students to read the first two stanzas and comment on them, I finally exhaled, but as silently as I could, as Mrs. Bridges maintained her post next to my desk. In a minute or so she began to walk slowly up the aisle to the front of the room as she listened to the struggling student. She sat down at her desk and continued to listen to the very tortured explanation of the verse.

I envisioned my 1949 Dodge as another one of my hapless fellow students struggled with the meaning of the next stanza of the poem. I could see Gloria running out the front door of her house and hugging me as I held the passenger door open for her. I could see us speeding off down the street as Martin frowned, powerless to keep us from leaving. And then I could see Mrs. Bridges staring down the aisle, her eyes shifting back and forth from Junior to me and back again. "Please read the next stanza and tell the class what you think it may mean," she said. I didn't even know which stanza we were on and was about to humiliate myself by asking, when she spoke again. "Please, James, go ahead."

Junior sat up a little straighter and began to read. "When the stars threw down their spears / And water'd heaven with their tears / Did he smile his work to see? / Did he who made the lamb make thee?" Junior looked up from his book and noisily cleared his throat. "I read this over several times and I have to admit that I'm not really sure what that means, especially the part about the stars watering heaven with tears."

Mrs. Bridges smiled. "That's all right, James, you are not alone. But, just tell me how you reacted to it—what thoughts you had or how it made you feel when you read it. I think sometimes we react to a poem on a gut level, but we think our reaction is somehow wrong or that the poem is just too complicated for us to understand. I don't want any of you to be afraid of poetry, or think that you aren't bright enough to understand it."

Junior remained silent and there were a few suppressed but audible starts of laughter. And then I heard someone whisper, "Yeah, don't be afraid, Junior."

"Would someone else like to answer?" Mrs. Bridges said. The room was silent again.

"Well," Junior said at last, "I felt that the poet was talking about all the good and evil in the world and that he wondered if the same creator could have given us both—the tiger and the lamb—the killer and the victim." Junior stopped at that point.

"Yes, please go on. Was there something more you wanted to say?"

"Well, I think the poet is also asking if the creator was happy with what he had done. He had created a world in which innocent creatures are killed by the stronger and more powerful creatures—where the weak are at the mercy of the strong, and the strong really show no mercy at all. At least, that's what I thought he was saying."

Junior stopped at that point and Mrs. Bridges just stared at him and gave no reaction to what he had said. I thought possibly Junior had completely misunderstood the poem and she was thinking of some kind way to correct him. She set her book down on her desk. "So the poet sees a world in which aggression or evil can prevail—where raw power rules—and then wonders if this almighty creator can possibly be happy with having made such a world, a world without mercy. And does the poet answer his own question?"

"No," Junior said without hesitation. "He asks the question, but he doesn't give an answer. When I read it, I felt that he wanted us to think about the question, but he wasn't going to tell us what we should conclude."

Mrs. Bridges stood up and walked around the front of her desk. "Thank you very much, James. Thank you." She lowered her head, her hands clasped in front of her waist, the book behind her on her desk. There was a long pause before she looked up and spoke again. "I think you did a fine job of understanding not only what this poet is saying to us, but also realizing the beauty and value of literature. The question this poet raises was not only valid in his time—it is still valid today. The question of how and why evil exists in this world is one that philosophers and theologians have struggled with for centuries. And these are the kind of questions that literature and poetry will bring before you. These are life questions that, sooner or later, we find we all confront in one way or another. What I hope you will learn in this class this year is that great writers experienced the same sort of desires and joy and pain and sorrows that we all experience. And that part of the beauty of literature is that these writers can reach across the years and touch you and let you know that you are not alone in this life." Mrs. Bridges stopped to smile at all of us. It was a sort of apologetic smile, as if, in her enthusiasm, she had gotten just a little ahead of the curriculum, or at least the lesson for the day. She walked to the row of desks across the aisle from Junior and stood in front of the first desk.

"There is something else I want you all to know, and that is that you are capable of great things. Yes, you are," she said emphatically. "There is no limit to what you can achieve, if you put your mind and heart into it and believe in yourself. Three years ago there was a student who sat at this very desk," she said and tapped the front desk with her right hand. "He was just like you—no different. Today, he is a cadet at the United States Military Academy at West Point. He was a South High student, and he sat right here," she repeated and tapped the desk again. "If there is an opportunity this year, I hope that he may stop back and speak to all of you."

When class ended, I caught up with Junior just as he was leaving the room. "I didn't know if she was calling on you or me to read that fifth stanza. I am so glad it was you, because I had completely lost track of where we were at."

"Really?"

"Yeah. And hey, quite a different message than the one we got last year from Mr. Horton."

Junior turned to look at me as we stepped into the hallway. A smile crossed his broad face. "Yeah, it sure is different. It kind of makes you wonder how they can be teaching at the same school."

Eighteen

My father and I went to the station where Tom worked and looked at the Dodge. He checked the engine and the tires and talked with Tom about its service record. He had me drive it around the neighborhood and then he drove it himself. When we returned the car to the station, my father circled slowly around the car several times in an apparent final inspection. After what seemed an interminable wait, he announced that he thought it was a "damned good car." He lectured me on when I would be able to use the car and how it could not interfere with my studies and that I would need to pay my own insurance, a repeat of conditions he had already outlined and an unnecessary and slightly humiliating experience as he delivered the speech in front of Tom. Somehow, it seemed, he always found a way to remove the joy from things. The owner was contacted and after a brief series of negotiations, I was able to purchase the car for two hundred and ten dollars. I was, finally, the owner of a car.

After I washed and waxed the car, my first priority was to contact Gloria and find a time when she could go for a ride. As it turned out, we both had the following Tuesday evening free and planned to get together immediately after dinner. I knew our date would be brief because it was a school night, but that didn't detract from the excitement of taking her out in my own car. It would be just the two of us, at last, driving off into a new world of freedom.

I called her as soon as I had bolted down my dinner on Tuesday. Gloria answered the phone and said I could come over right away. There was some strange, raspy quality to her voice I could not decipher and her conversation was hurried. The brief call didn't seem to reflect at all the excitement and anticipation I knew we both had felt when I first told her about the car, and I was at a loss to understand what had happened. I hurried to leave the house, enduring another series of cautions and rules from both my parents as I tried to make my exit. I needed to be home by nine o'clock, because they knew there was homework to be done. I shouldn't do any "hot-rodding" with the car: no speeding, no drag racing, no running through amber lights, no ignoring stop signs, no quick starts or squealing of tires. I answered yes to every order directed at me and nodded my head to emphasize how clearly and profoundly I understood and agreed with each instruction.

In less than ten minutes I was approaching Gloria's house. As I began to near the curb, I saw that Gloria was already standing in the front yard waiting for me. She ran to the car as I approached, opened the passenger door, dropped into the seat and slammed the door. "God," she rasped, "please get me out of here."

I looked at her briefly before I pulled away from the curb. She was staring straight ahead, her face tense, her mouth pulled tight in anger. "What's going on, Gloria? What are you so upset about?"

"Sorry, Will. Thanks for picking me up," she said, and as a sudden afterthought, "And I love your car. It's great, really. It looks so clean." She took time to look around the interior, paused to smile at me and then began to stare out the windshield again.

I turned on the radio and tuned it to WDGY, but kept the volume low. The station was playing Buddy Holly tunes in a retrospective celebrating his work. "So, what's going on?"

"It's Martin. He's a pig and I hate him."

"Yeah, what happened?"

Gloria lowered her head and sniffed twice. When she spoke again her voice was shaky, as if she were trying to keep from crying. "Do you remember the last time you were over and I told you there was more I wanted to tell you about him?"

"Yes," I said and strained to keep my attention on negotiating the street and the next intersection. The autumn sun was brilliant in a cloudless sky and the canopy of gold and yellow and orange leaves appeared to glow with the early evening light. Now this perfect afternoon was somehow being threatened by Martin Scully.

Gloria lifted her head and looked out the windshield again. When she spoke, her voice was no longer shaky, but calm and even. "Well, what I wanted to tell you was that he . . ."

I glanced to see if she was crying, but all I could see was the hard etchings of anger on her face. "He what?"

"He stares at me all the time—well, not all the time, just when my mom isn't around."

"He stares at you?" I knew what she meant and a mixture of anger and anxiety swept over me. I could feel my heart beat faster.

"Yeah, it's been going on for a year or so and the other day he gave me this playful little swat on the butt, except it wasn't playful at all. I wanted to rip his damn hand off and hit him with it."

"What did you do?"

"I slapped his hand away and gave him the dirtiest look I've ever given anyone. He doesn't fool me, and I want him to know it. But today was the worst yet."

I tried not to take my eyes off the road, but I could barely concentrate on driving. "What happened today?"

"I took a shower after dinner. When I was drying off, I noticed the door was open just a crack, and I knew I had closed it tight. And then I saw his filthy little eyes peeking through the crack at me."

"Shit," I said, my thoughts and emotions in tumult. "What did you do?"

"I slammed the door so hard that if he'd been any closer he would have had a broken nose." There was no longer any trace of tearfulness, just a white-hot anger in her voice.

My thoughts raced and shifted, like the discordant drumming of a hundred nervous fingers. "You've got to do something about that guy. I think you need to tell your mom about it—all of it. You can't live with a guy like that. I mean, who knows what he might do?"

"I don't know, Will. It's so damn hard." The anger was gone from her voice, now replaced by a sort of melancholy resignation. "She loves the guy, or thinks she does. I've thought and thought about it and I don't know what I should do. I guess I just want to get out of there."

She fell silent as I continued along the streets, the Dodge rolling through the corridor of autumn trees and dappled sunlight. I tried to keep visions of Martin out of my thoughts, without success. I kept seeing his dark, sinister face and imagining him leering after Gloria. I felt a sudden urge to stop somewhere and get out and walk with Gloria in the late afternoon sun, to escape the confines of the car and the persistent images of Martin Scully. "Would you like to go out to the falls and take a walk?"

"That would be nice," Gloria whispered.

I headed southeast toward Minnehaha Falls. Neither of us spoke as we continued along the tree-lined boulevards that led to the falls. As soon as I had parked, I got out and opened Gloria's door and the two of us walked hand-in-hand to a waist-high stone wall and looked out at the falls. The flow of Minnehaha creek was strong and full as it fell more than fifty feet to crash and foam on the rocky ledge below. We watched for a moment or two. Still, neither of us said a word. Then I led her along the wall to the stone steps that curved down to the base of the falls and the continuation of the sinuous creek. There was no one in sight as we walked to the stone footbridge that crossed over the creek. We stopped in the middle of the bridge to watch the swiftly flowing water beneath us and look up at the thundering falls. I put my arm across Gloria's back and pulled her close to me. She nestled into my one-armed embrace and then I turned her toward me and encircled her with my arms. She held up her face like an expectant child. I put one hand behind her head and pulled her face toward mine so I could whisper in her ear and know that my voice could be heard above the rushing creek and the roar of the falls. "I love you," I said. I said it without any thought of how she might react or whether or not it was the right time to say such a thing or even if I understood all of what that really meant.

She threw her arms around my neck and held on tight. "I love you, too," she said.

* * * * *

It was nearly dark by the time we left the falls. I wanted to be sure Gloria would be home on time. I also wanted to speak to Martin Scully. Gloria sat beside me, her head leaning against her window, her face looking relaxed and untroubled. I hated to disturb her, but there were things I needed to know before our time together ended. "Are you afraid of him?" I said.

Gloria was so peaceful and relaxed that she seemed in a trance-like state. "What?" she said dreamily.

"Are you afraid of Martin? I have to know."

She sat up and turned toward me. "Afraid?" There was a pause before she spoke again, as if she needed to give her answer careful consideration. "No, I'm not afraid of him. I think he's a coward and a liar." Another pause. "No, I'm not afraid of him."

I was glad she wasn't fearful, but that wasn't enough. "I want to stop in for a minute when we get to your house. Okay?"

"Sure, but why do you want to stop in?"

"I have an idea. It's kind of crazy, I guess, but it might help things. I just want to talk to Martin for a minute or so. Just go along with what I say. Okay?"

Gloria slid across the seat and grabbed my arm so forcefully that the car lurched to the right for an instant before I straightened the steering wheel again. "Sounds pretty mysterious, Will. What's going on?"

"It's just a thought I had. I don't know, it might be dumb, but I want to try and make the guy think a little about how he acts around you. I hate the thought of him even being in the same house with you."

Gloria held on tight to my arm. "I'll be okay, Will."

* * * * *

When we got to Gloria's house, Martin and her mother were in the living room sitting on opposite ends of the couch watching TV. When Gloria's mother saw me she immediately got up. "Will, come in." She hurried across the room. "Come in. It's so good to see you again."

"Nice to see you too, Mrs. Scully, but I'm afraid I can't stay. I just wanted to say hello to you and Mr. Scully. I have to get home myself."

Martin Scully looked up but didn't speak to me or make any effort to rise from the couch.

"Well, I really have to go. Good to see you all again." I started back toward the front door, as Gloria and her mother followed close behind me. I turned back to Martin. "Oh, Mr. Scully, I meant to ask you if you happen to know my uncle." I hoped my voice would not betray my nervousness.

Martin looked up from the couch, a scowl on his face. "What?"

"My uncle, Dave Ross—I think you might know him. He said he stops in your butcher shop now and then. He's a big guy, kind of loud. He's a Minneapolis cop, works in the sex crimes division. Do you know him?"

The scowl left Martin's face. His eyes widened slightly. "Your uncle's a cop?"

"Yeah, Dave Ross. I see him a lot and I mentioned you to him. He thought he knew you from the shop where you work." I tried to sound breezy and matter-of-fact.

"I don't . . . I don't think so."

"That's funny. I'm sure you'd remember him. He's about six-foot-five and has this big voice. Oh, well, maybe he was thinking of one of the other butchers."

"Yeah, maybe," he said. His voice sounded distant and tenuous.

"Well, gotta go. It was good to see you all again." I opened the front door. Gloria followed me out the door while her mother bent down and caught Josephine before she could make an escape. She scooped up the cat and headed back toward the living room while Gloria walked out to the car with me. "Stop back sometime when you can visit," Gloria's mother called out over her shoulder.

"I'll do that," I shouted back.

"None of that was true, was it?" Gloria whispered as we reached my car.

"Well, I do have an uncle."

"Oh, Will," she said and forced a little laugh. "You were very convincing."

"Listen to me, Gloria. If that guy ever touches you again, I want you to tell me about it. If he tries to sneak another look at you, I want you to tell me about it. I'm serious."

She looked down at the ground for a moment and then raised her eyes to mine. "I know you're serious."

"Then promise me. If he does anything at all, you'll tell me."

"I promise, Will."

"Okay. Goodnight," I said as I kissed her quickly on the forehead and glanced back at the house. I couldn't see anyone in the picture window, only the shifting glow of the television in the darkened living room.

I was about to step into my car and close the door when Gloria called out to me. "I loved my first ride in your car."

"There'll be lots more."

"Thanks for everything, Will." She waved as I pulled out from the curb. I looked in my rearview mirror as I drove away. I could see her still standing in the yard watching me, her arms folded across her midsection as she hunched against the chill of the evening.

Nineteen

"So, how's that Dodge working out for you?" Tom said as we pulled away from my house.

"I think it's a great car. I haven't had any problems at all."

A cigarette dangled from his mouth as he punched the lighter on the dash. "Yeah, well, don't forget to check the oil every time you stop for gas."

"Yes, Mother."

Tom laughed. "How does Gloria like the car?" He glanced at me as he spoke.

"She likes it too. You know girls. It's not that big a deal to her."

"Uh-huh," Tom grunted. "Hey, you heard about what happened to Rick Madison after school the other day, right?" His mood was now devoid of all humor.

"Yeah, I heard about it." He was referring to a fight that had taken place two days earlier. In reality, it had been more of a beating than a fight. Rick had somehow angered and insulted Anthony Johnson. After school, Anthony had beaten Rick so badly that both of Rick's eyes were swollen shut and he had needed stitches to close a cut on his chin. At least that was the story that had gone around school the following day when Rick didn't show up for classes. The fact that Anthony was black and Rick was white gave the fight an emotional aspect that would otherwise not have existed. "What about it?"

Tom held the steering wheel with his left hand as he flicked cigarette ash into the tray on the dash. He stomped down on the accelerator as the amber light changed to red. We raced through the intersection as cars to our left and right honked in protest. "God, Tom, take it easy, will you?"

"You don't think this shit is getting a little out of hand?"

"You mean your driving?"

"I mean it, Will. Rick is this little guy and Anthony just beats the crap out of him for no reason—other than maybe the fact that he's white."

"You know, Tom, the truth is, I don't really know what happened—and neither do you."

"Yeah? Well, it doesn't take a genius to know Rick got his ass kicked because Anthony thought it would be fun to tromp on some little white guy."

"Oh, man." I said with disgust and looked out my window. The sun was going down, dipping just below the rooftops. The trees had lost most of their leaves in a recent heavy rain, and now their tops had become a web of lacy, charcoal silhouettes against a gray and mauve sky. I watched the roofs and treetops float past my window. I looked at the square little houses and the chain-link fences and the damp, leaf-strewn sidewalks. As Tom turned right and headed south on Hiawatha Avenue, I lit a cigarette. I took a deep drag and leaned back and closed my eyes. I tried not to think about fights and beatings and the pulse of anger and hatred that seemed to drum a relentless rhythm in Tom's life.

"You think I'm wrong?" Tom asked as he turned into the gravel lot of Beek's Pizza, under the crown-shaped sign that declared "Beek—King of Pizza."

"I don't know, Tom. I just . . . I guess I just don't want to think about that right now."

"Fine," Tom said as he pulled up next to a green Mercury.

"Isn't that Pipsqueak's car?" I said.

"Sure looks like it."

We walked to the entry, where we could hear the high-pitched, piercing laughter of young girls even before Tom opened the door. Only about half the tables were taken, but the staff behind the counter were busy opening and closing oven doors and cutting up pizzas. Tom and I took a table in a corner, where we could see anyone who entered or exited. It was warm inside the shack and I put my windbreaker over the back of my chair. I picked a menu out from between a napkin holder and peppershaker on the bare table. I hadn't really felt hungry until we were inside and I could smell the baking pizzas. Now I couldn't wait to eat. Tom stood behind his chair as I scanned the menu.

"Why don't we split a large pepperoni?" he said as he looked around the room.

"Sounds good to me," I said and put the menu back on the table.

"I see Pipsqueak. I'm going to go talk to him for a second. I'll be right back."

I watched Tom cross the room. Pipsqueak was sitting with several girls, his back to Tom's approach. The girls all laughed uproariously at something Pipsqueak said. Just before Tom reached the table, Pipsqueak turned to greet him as the girls fell silent. He smiled at Tom and stood to shake his hand. They spoke for a second or two, and then Pipsqueak looked in my direction and waved. I waved back. "Hello, Pipsqueak," I mumbled to no one.

"Do you know what you'd like?" A squatty waitress stood to my left, one hip thrust to the side, a pencil poised above a small pad. She didn't look at me, but gazed intently at her order pad.

"Yes. We'd like a large pepperoni—and sausage—pizza, and a pitcher of Coke."

She made a hurried note on the tablet. "Is that all?"

"How much does a guy have to eat around here?" I said and laughed.

She struck the pad with her pencil, glanced at me and marched away.

After a few minutes, Tom returned. "Did you order?" he said as he sat down across from me.

"Yeah. Hey, what's the deal with Pipsqueak and all the girls?"

Tom looked back over his shoulder at Pipsqueak's table. "They're just tooling him for his car and his money. He's not exactly Errol Flynn. Who do you think is paying for all the pizza at their table?"

"That's real nice."

Tom shook his head and smiled. "You think Pipsqueak doesn't understand what's going on? Hell, he's fine with all of it. They get free rides and pizza, and Pipsqueak gets to hang out with the pretty ladies and look like a big shot. Everybody's happy."

"Really?"

"That's right, Will. I'll tell you something else: it keeps going like that your whole life." Tom leaned back and lit a cigarette, a satisfied grin on his face.

"So everything is a trade-off, eh, Tom?"

Tom took a long drag on his cigarette and let the smoke roll up from his mouth into his nostrils. He blew two smoke rings, one inside the other. "That's right, Will. That's how the world works. I learned that a long time ago."

"Maybe not always," I said. I wanted to say more, but I knew nothing I could say would change his attitude, so I let it go.

Our Coke arrived, and shortly afterward the large pizza. Tom mashed out his cigarette. We each pulled pieces from either side of the tray. In my hurry to bite into my first piece, I managed to swing some of the hot mozzarella cheese onto my lower lip. "Ah—shit!"

Tom laughed. "See, Will—trade-offs. You have to let the pizza cool before you get to eat it."

"Funny, Tom," I said as I reached for my drink. I rolled the icy glass back and forth against my lip.

Tom leaned forward, his voice low and confidential. "Hey, listen. I think when we get done here we're going to take a little ride over to Elliot Park."

Elliot Park was several miles away, on the near south side of downtown Minneapolis. "Elliot Park, what the hell for?"

He didn't answer immediately, but took his time chewing on his piece of pizza. When he was done with the slice, he snatched one of the paper napkins from the holder and slowly wiped his hands and mouth. Then he sat back and looked at me intently, the napkin still in his right hand. "Pipsqueak told me there's going to be a little settling of accounts at the park tonight."

"What? What are you talking about?"

"Some people are getting together to see that the score gets evened up for Rick Madison."

I sat back, stunned by what he had said. "Who are 'some people'?"

Tom named a couple of seniors and several former students of South High, all with widely known reputations as badasses. Some had served time at the St. Cloud Reformatory, or "The Clouds" as it was known on the street. "We'll just check it out. See what's going on."

"No, Tom. Not this time. I'm not going to Elliot Park to find out if I can get my skull busted open for some insane idea of justice."

Tom leaned forward. "Hey, don't go nuts on me. I just said we'd check it out."

"Look, Tom, I know what that means. We'll go to the park and get right into the middle of whatever's happening. It's stupid—and we could get our asses kicked."

Tom picked up another piece of pizza and settled back into his chair. He watched me as he chewed his food. He was nearly finished with his slice before he spoke again. "I remember a time when you were fine with someone helping to even things up for you." He continued to look at me as he wiped his mouth with the crumpled napkin in his right hand. He took a drink of his Coke. "Think about that."

His reference was to a fight that had taken place when we were in seventh grade. One of the biggest eighth grade kids at Holy Rosary had threatened me throughout the day. He had promised to "get me" for some imagined offense. I was scared, and everyone knew it. When a crowd gathered after school, Tom stepped forward to defend me. He told the bigger boy he would need to deal with him before he ever touched me. The boy ignored Tom's warning and suffered a bloody nose and a humbling defeat as a result. He had never bothered Tom or me again. "We were kids, Tom. It isn't the same thing at all. For God's sake, you have no idea what might happen at that park tonight. This isn't some schoolyard bully getting his nose bloodied."

"Yeah, well, I happen to think it is the same thing."

"No," I said, "it really isn't. You know what it is? You know what it really is? It's the same kind of stupid crap that Junior Kandowski was able to stop last year after football practice. Remember that? Remember how all the colored and white guys were ready to kill each other—and then Junior walked out with Sonny Holmes and everything stopped. It's that same kind of brainless crap that will bring people to Elliot Park tonight. Rick's white and Anthony is colored, so let's all fight." My voice betrayed my agitation.

Tom looked down at the pizza. He pulled another slice away and held it over his plate. "Fine, Will, don't go. When we're done here, I'll drop you at your house and go to the park by myself."

I exhaled and tried to find some way to calm myself. I took another breath, and another. "Tom, come on," I said slowly. "Don't do that. Don't make it a test of our friendship."

"Who said anything about it being a test of our friendship?"

"Tom, look, I'm not . . . I just don't see this the way you do."

"Yeah, that's obvious," he said, his tone dismissive.

I thought about all the years we had known each other, and how we had been as close as brothers from the very start, but now seemed to be on divergent paths. I couldn't name the hour or the day or the week that it began, but we were being pulled in different directions. I didn't want that to continue. And yet, I felt that any chance to change things between us might already be slipping out of my grasp. "Tom, can I tell you something?"

"Shoot."

I struggled to find the right words. "We've been friends forever, and that means a lot to me. I know you've taken risks for me and taken my side in everything—you've always done that. I couldn't have a better friend."

"Yeah, but?"

"I just . . . I don't know how to put it. I know that you've had to deal with a lot of stuff that I haven't, and I think it has made you . . . I don't know. It's like you're mad at everything and everybody. I just don't feel that way, Tom. I've just never gone in much for hating people." I was sorry immediately for what I had said. It was more harsh than I intended and unfair, but I had said it.

Tom gave me a piercing stare, and then dropped what was left of his piece of pizza on his plate. He took a long drink from his glass of Coke, then set the glass back on the table and wiped his mouth with the same crumpled, greasy napkin. "Hey, it's not a problem," he said evenly, the dismissive tone gone from his voice, replaced by a quiet resignation. "You're right, Will, we do see things differently. Maybe you're right, maybe I'm right. Who knows? Anyway, don't worry about it. We're friends. That doesn't get wiped out because of one argument."

Somehow, everything he said made me feel that I had failed in what I was trying to explain. "Tom . . ." I began again.

"Hey," he said, "don't turn into Will the Worrier on me." He reached across the table and delivered an awkward punch to my shoulder.

* * * * *

TWENTY MINUTES LATER, TOM DROPPED ME OFF at my house. The sun had gone down, and there was a chill in the air and the pungent smell of damp, rotting leaves. I got out of the car, held the door open and ducked my head back into the front seat. "You still plan on going to the park?"

Tom smiled and gunned his engine slightly. "I think maybe I'll just take a look."

I shook my head. "Damn it, Tom, don't do it. Okay?"

He gunned the engine again. "I'll think about it—Mom."

There was nothing more to say. "I'll see you, Tom."

"Yeah. See ya."

I closed the door. Tom immediately hit the gas. The drive wheel squealed against the pavement, and the car fishtailed as he drove away. I watched the car disappear into the darkened corridor of the street, only the red taillights visible as he made a left turn at the end of the block.

Twenty

THERE WAS NO FIGHT AT ELLIOT PARK. Tom told me that when he got there, he saw five cars parked along the southern border of the park, each with four or five white boys inside. There were at least an equal number of black kids milling around the nearby picnic tables and wading pool. He also saw a KSTP television van at the curb on the same side of the park, and two police squads moving into the area. Tom had maintained a steady speed, took the first available turn and headed away from the park. I was glad nothing had happened, but I also felt it was only a delay of the brutality that wove with persistence through Tom's life.

I had tried to deny it at first, but I knew we were at a critical juncture in our friendship. More and more I found I wanted to avoid being out with Tom, because the potential for violence was always present. It was there at a party, or when we went out to eat, or even in the most casual encounters with strangers. I wasn't certain if violence inexplicably gravitated toward him, or if it was something he sought out as naturally as a flame consumes oxygen. But if I couldn't change the course of things, it didn't matter. And for all of this I felt guilty. Just how much did I owe him? How persuasive could I hope to be in any attempt to change the way he saw life? How long could my loyalty last if he was beyond any influence to change? And so one evening when the phone rang in the next room, I said to my mother, "If that's Tom, tell him I'm not home." When I turned, Tom was standing at the back entry. The interior door was open slightly, with only a screen between us.

"Tom, I didn't know you were . . . there," I said, stumbling over the words from the shock of his presence. I tried not to show my embarrassment about what I had just said, and hoped against all logic that he hadn't heard me.

He stared at me for a moment before he spoke. "So, what are you doing tonight?" he said at last. I wasn't sure if he was ignoring what I had said to my mother or if he had somehow truly failed to hear me.

"I was going to head over to Gloria's," I lied.

"Okay," he said. "I just thought I would drop by and see if you maybe wanted to cruise around for awhile."

I felt certain now that he had heard me. His demeanor was so subdued and uncertain, as if something in the world had finally found a way to wound him. "Well, I mean, it isn't really like a date or anything," I said, angry with myself for lying to him. "I mean, we could go out for a while."

Tom backed away from the door. "No, no, it's okay. Forget it, Will. Another time." He raised his right hand to his hip level in a sort of half-wave and hurried away from the door and down the steps to his car.

"Tom," I called out, but he was already gone.

"What was that all about?" my mother said as she came back into the kitchen.

"What?"

"I thought Gloria was working tonight. Didn't you just tell Tom you were going over there? And why did you want him to think you weren't home?"

"Never mind, Mom." I spat the words, lashing out at her with displaced anger. I turned away before she could speak, walked heavy-footed to my bedroom and slammed the door.

* * * * *

I DIDN'T SEE OR HEAR FROM TOM for the next two days. At work on Sunday afternoon, while I was alone in the kitchen with little to do, I kept turning the incident over in my mind. I thought about apologizing to him, but then wondered if maybe he really hadn't heard anything—or maybe it would all pass in time, no matter what he had heard. I was considering these possibilities when Jim emerged from his basement slumber and began to inspect the readiness of the kitchen for the dinner hour.

He checked the vat of boiling chicken stock, glanced at the grills and the deep fryers and then began lifting each of the hoods on the steam table. "Everything looks good," he said as he continued to amble toward me. "Much business this afternoon?"

"Not really. It's been pretty quiet."

"Yeah? Well, that's all right," he said, as if the god of money couldn't be expected to visit incessantly.

"I got the walk-in freezer all cleaned up, changed the grease in the fryers and cleaned the grills."

"Yeah, it all looks good." He didn't leave for his usual smoke break in the corner, but leaned his elbows against the counter and looked out through the serving window toward the dining room. "You're going to be a senior next year, right?"

"Yeah, if I make it through my junior year," I joked.

He ignored my half-hearted attempt at humor. "Have you thought about what you want to do after you graduate?" He continued to lean on the counter and gaze at the dining room. He clasped his hands together, like a man in a church pew as he readied himself for prayer.

"Well, not really. I've thought about maybe going into the Army."

"Yeah? I was in the Army. Not much of a life, if you ask me."

"Well, I mean just for a couple of years, and maybe then decide if I want to go to school or something."

He maintained his prayer-like posture and continued to look toward the dining room. "You know, being a cook can be a damned good life. I don't mean crap like this short-order stuff you're doing now. I'm talking about being a chef in a top hotel or restaurant. You can make damn good money."

I didn't have the heart to tell him that I wasn't particularly interested in cooking or becoming a chef. I wasn't certain what I wanted to do after high school, but I had some idea of what I didn't want to do. "Yeah, I guess," I said.

Jim pulled back from the counter, stretched his arms overhead and yawned as he stood up straight, and then turned toward me. He folded his arms across his chest and looked at me, his gray eyes unblinking. "I can teach you a few things here, but you'd really need to go to a good vocational school, take up hotel and restaurant cooking." He looked around the kitchen, surveying the steam table and sandwich board, the grills and fryers, the chopping table and the sinks. "Of course, this isn't a bad living, either. You know, I originally hired Matt thinking he could take over when I retired," he said, referring to my middle-aged co-worker. "He just couldn't handle it. He came to me one day nearly in tears and said he just couldn't handle the ordering and menu planning and all the other crap that goes with it, so I said fine. 'Fine,' I said, 'you don't have to learn all that.' I told him he was welcome to stay and just do the short-order stuff and dish up dinners, if that was what he wanted to do. So, here he is, nearly fifteen years later, doing the same thing you're doing."

"Oh, I didn't know all that."

"Yeah," he said. He unfolded his arms and brushed some imaginary crumbs from the counter. "Yeah, I don't know," he said, his voice full of weariness. "I think maybe it's too late for me to find someone to break in on this place now. The owner, old man Keller, he'll have to figure out what he wants to do when I leave here. I think it's too late now.

"But you, you've got your life ahead of you. You could go to school and learn the business the right way. Get into some fancy hotel and be a chef. That's where the real bucks are." He stared beyond me at some point in the distance, no longer giving expression to whatever thoughts stirred behind his tired eyes.

"Yeah," I said, and hoped he was done with talk of cooking and my future. "I guess that's really worth considering. I'm just not sure what I want to do after school. Not yet, anyway."

Jim continued to stare off into the distance and didn't react to what I'd said. I thought at any moment he would likely leave for a cigarette break, but instead he walked to one of the fryers, checked the temperature setting and then turned back to me. "Did I tell you that Bea and I got burial plots over at Lakewood Cemetery?"

This moribund turn in our conversation caught me by surprise. "No . . . I . . . no, I had no idea."

"Yeah, two plots, side by side. It's a beautiful spot. They're on a slight rise, not a hill, really, but just a nice, gentle rise. There's a tree there—an old red maple—just above the plots. And the plots look out over the lake." He picked up one of the fryer baskets and shook it. He looked the basket over carefully and then hooked it back on top of the deep fryer. "A real peaceful spot."

"It sounds very nice," I said. I didn't know what else to say.

"Yeah. That's where we'll spend our rest—on that gentle, grassy rise, looking out over the lake."

I was more confused than ever about Jim's philosophical view of life and concept of eternity. He apparently envisioned Bea and himself existing in some sort of lakeside paradise, forever gazing out over the grassy slope at the lake beyond, in a state of eternal bliss under the shadow of an old maple tree. I wondered how all this meshed with his concept of God as money, and his departure from the Catholic Church and its teachings about the miracle of the virgin birth. To me, it was all such an incredible hodgepodge of unrelated abstractions that I couldn't imagine getting any sort of rational grasp on his beliefs. I had no idea where I would even begin to question him, if that was what I had wanted to do. And then he rescued me from my musings.

"Well, I'm going to go grab a smoke. Just give me a holler if it gets busy."

"Okay, Jim. Thanks."

He was nearly to the break table when he stopped and turned to speak to me. "Say, I've been meaning to ask you, are you still seeing that young lady you took out on the Fourth of July? What was her name?"

"Gloria. Gloria Jensen. Yes, I'm still seeing her."

"So you two are getting along fine?"

"Yes, we are."

He smiled and nodded several times. He removed his cook's hat and wiped his brow with his forearm. He looked at the newly dampened spot on the white sleeve of his chef's jacket and put the hat back on his head. "That's good. I'm glad to hear it," he said, and then he turned and continued on.

Twenty-One

At midweek in early November, I was going to take Gloria out for dinner. There was nothing elaborate about our plans, just a burger or pizza somewhere. We had talked over the weekend about getting together, both of us excited at the prospect of having a few hours alone. After I had gotten home from school, stashed my books in my bedroom and assured my parents I wouldn't be out late, I slipped on my tanker jacket and picked up the phone to let Gloria know I was on my way.

My call was answered on the second ring. "Hello?"

"Gloria, it's me. I'm leaving now. I'll be there in five minutes."

There was no response at first, just a scraping sound, as if something was being drawn across the mouthpiece of the phone. "This is Gloria's mother, Will."

"Oh. Hi, Mrs. Scully. I thought you were Gloria. Could you tell her that I'll be right over?"

Again, there was no immediate response. I could hear what sounded like muffled voices, one of them high and staccato. The voices alternated, first the lower, calmer sounding voice and then the counterpoint of high, rapid outbursts. I strained to make out what was being said, but couldn't understand any of the words. The indistinct voices stopped and Mrs. Scully cleared her throat before she spoke again. "I'm afraid Gloria doesn't want to see you tonight, Will."

At first I thought I must have misunderstood what she had said. "What? I don't understand . . . What did you say?"

My voice must have betrayed my shock and anxiety, as my father lowered his evening paper and looked at me, his brow furrowed. I turned my back to my father and faced the corner of the room. I made an effort to sound unconcerned and matter-of-fact.

"I don't understand. We're supposed to go out tonight. Why doesn't she want to see me?"

"I'm afraid you'll have to talk with her about that another time, Will. This is between the two of you, that's all I can say."

"Can I talk to her?" I strained to keep my voice low and measured.

"I'm sorry, Will. She doesn't want to talk to you."

I could feel my heart race and my breathing become quick and shallow. "Well, all right then," I said as cheerfully as I could manage, "I'll be over in a few minutes."

"No, Will, I don't think you should do that."

"Okay, see you," I said and hung up.

I set the phone back in its cradle and turned to leave. My father lowered his paper again and stared at me. "Something wrong?"

"No. Just a little mix-up for a second, everything's fine. I'm heading over to Gloria's now. I'll be back before nine."

He lifted the newspaper back to its reading position and gave it a perfunctory shake. "Be sure you are."

* * * * *

THE SKY WAS OVERCAST AND THE STREETS, houses, and barren trees seemed a colorless patchwork of gray and black. I looked through the windshield of the Dodge up at the leaden sky as I turned the key in the ignition. I could hear the engine straining, but it failed to start. I released the key, pumped the gas pedal twice and tried again. Again the engine failed to fire. "What the hell is going on," I said aloud, realizing as I spoke the words that I was thinking of both Gloria and the Dodge. "Come on, come on." I pumped the gas again, and on the third try the engine started. It was when I shifted into first gear that I noticed my hands were shaking.

I drove along the streets to Gloria's house with only a remote awareness of what I was doing. It wasn't until I stopped at a red light on Cedar Avenue that I realized my location and understood I had reached this point with no memory of having left my house or having driven the last five blocks. All my thoughts were of Gloria and her mysterious refusal to see me or talk to me. I wondered if something nightmarish was unfolding that involved Martin Scully. As I watched the red light, several drops of rain struck the windshield—one, two, three. Why would she refuse to talk to me? Four, five. Why didn't she want to see me? The raindrops began to turn to snow, little slushy droplets that stuck in place momentarily and then melted away and ran in crooked streams down the glass. The red light changed to green and I hit the gas with unintentional force. I felt the Dodge sway beneath me as I shot away.

Within minutes I pulled up in front of Gloria's house. The mix of rain and snow had stopped for the moment. As I climbed out of the car, I noticed a sudden movement of color in my peripheral vision, darting from the house into the yard. I turned to see Gloria rushing toward my car. She was wearing a bright pink, cable-knit sweater and charcoal slacks. She hurried toward the car, her arms wrapped across her midsection. She stopped within twenty feet of the car. As I began to walk around the front of the Dodge, she screamed something, her voice ragged and unfamiliar to me. I slowed my pace. "What?" I called out to her.

She took a step or two backward and hollered at me for a second time. "You went out with Jean O'Hara?"

I stopped in front of the car. "What?" I said again, stunned by her raging, plaintive cry and the content of her question. "Who told you that?"

She took another step backward and held herself tightly around the waist. "It's true then, isn't it?"

For a moment, I had no idea how to respond. I noticed Gloria's mother standing at the front entry, watching us from behind the glass of the storm door. Snow began to fall again, heavy wet flakes that stuck to the shoulders of Gloria's sweater and her hair. A single flake caught on an eyelash and flickered at me as she blinked her eyes. She was trembling now, and little streams of moisture ran down her cheeks, tears and snowmelt mingling on her face. "It wasn't what you think," I said. I stepped onto the lawn and began to walk toward her.

Gloria backed away from me. "How could you? How could you?" she screamed. She spat the words out, her scream trailing into tears and a low moaning sound. "Oh, God," she said, as if she were in physical pain. "Do you know what the other girls call her? Do you?"

"Gloria . . ."

"They call her Jean O'Whore-a. Pretty funny, huh, Will? My boyfriend went out with Jean O'Whore-a." She sobbed once and caught her breath quickly. "A moonlight swim, wasn't that it? Isn't that right?"

"Gloria, please let me explain. It wasn't what you think at all."

She held up one hand, palm extended toward me. "Stop," she shouted. She was shaking badly now, and her voice was loud and tremulous. "Oh, God," she moaned again and covered her mouth with her right hand. She stood like that for an instant, and then wrapped her arms about her waist again. "Leave me alone!" she screamed. "Just leave me alone!" Her face was flushed as she cried freely.

"Gloria, listen to me—" Before I could say anything more, she turned and ran back to her house. Her mother opened the storm door, all the while staring at me. Gloria rushed inside—and into the arms of her mother. Mrs. Scully continued to watch me as she hugged her daughter. I could see little convulsive movements of Gloria's back as she buried her face in her mother's shoulder. Mrs. Scully watched me, her gaze unbroken, and then she shook her head back and forth, signaling me to leave.

I stood and watched Gloria and her mother as the slushy flakes began to cover the grass and fallen leaves and sidewalk. I stood there, not knowing whether to go or stay. After a few moments, Gloria's mother closed the door to the house. I watched the lifeless house, still frozen by my indecision and shock. Somewhere down the street a dog began to bark. The barking continued in evenly spaced bursts, echoing along the cold, empty street. It was as if the harsh, intrusive sound made me realize there was nothing more I could do at the moment, so I walked back to my car and got inside. I sat behind the steering wheel and felt little chunks of slush melt and run in rivulets down my forehead and temples. My only thoughts were to find a way to make Gloria understand what had really happened, to make her realize I hadn't betrayed her. I wished Dee were home. She would know the best thing to do, I thought. And why had I listened to Tom? Why hadn't I told Gloria about that night at the lake as I had intended?

I started the car and slowly pulled away from the curb, not knowing where I should go. I couldn't go home, not yet anyway. I drove south, in the direction of home, but continued along Cedar Avenue toward Lake Street. I began to feel sick to my stomach as I recalled the times Gloria had told me she trusted me—and loved me. I saw her face the day she told me she would never marry someone she didn't trust—and then her face today, full of anguish and sorrow. I drove on, haunted by a jumble of memories that kept alternating between happy, tender moments and her tear-streaked face this afternoon and that horrible look of having been betrayed. I felt tears well up in my eyes. "God damn it!" I shouted and slammed both palms against the steering wheel. "You idiot," I shouted to no one. I had driven several blocks on Lake Street when I spotted a phone booth. I parked the car and walked back to the phone through the cold, slanting mix of rain and snow.

I dialed Gloria's number. By the fifth ring there was still no answer. I was about to hang up when Mrs. Scully came on the line. "This is Will," I said hurriedly. "Please, don't hang up. Please, just listen to me."

There was an ominous pause, and then, "Go ahead."

"Mrs. Scully, I know this looks terrible and like I went out with someone else behind Gloria's back, but it isn't like that at all. Last summer a friend of mine told a couple of girls we were going to meet them, but he didn't even tell me about it until I was already in the car." I could hear her breathing. When she exhaled, I read into that single sound her total disgust and disbelief in what I was saying. I felt she might, at any moment, slam down the phone. I tried to talk more quickly, convinced I had only seconds remaining before the connection would be broken. "I told the girl, Jean O'Hara, that Gloria was my girlfriend and that I wasn't interested in anyone else. I never even kissed her or anything, and that's the truth."

There was a long pause, and then Mrs. Scully's voice sounding low, with an edge of anger. "I don't know what all Gloria heard at school, Will. All I know is that I've never seen my daughter so broken hearted. She's in her room now crying. I've never seen her so hurt."

I could feel my face grow hot with embarrassment and sorrow over what I had done, and what I had failed to do. "Mrs. Scully, I swear to God I would never do anything to hurt Gloria. I need to make her understand that it was nothing—nothing happened. It was just stupid."

"Why didn't you tell her about it, Will? Why did you try and hide it from her if nothing happened?"

"I thought it wasn't important." I recalled Tom's advice to me, but knew in the end I was the one who had decided to follow that advice. "I guess I thought telling Gloria about it would just upset her over nothing."

There was another long pause. "You'll have to explain it to her yourself."

"But I can't explain it to her if she won't even listen to me. Will you please ask her to talk to me?"

"Not now, Will." She no longer sounded angry, but emotionally drained and weary.

"No, I understand. I don't mean now, but sometime. Could you please help me and maybe say she should at least let me explain?"

There was another long pause, so long that I was about to ask if she was still on the line. And then, at last, she spoke. "I don't know, Will. I'll have to think about it. I have to go now."

"Thank you so mu—" Before I could finish my sentence, I could hear the steady hum of the broken connection. I put the receiver back in its cradle and looked out of the booth at the few people hurrying along the avenue. A woman in a dark blue coat ran across Lake Street as the traffic light turned green. She hunched into the wind, her head down and turned against the relentless snow. A man dressed only in slacks and a shirt ducked quickly into a barbershop. The traffic along Lake Street was moving more slowly now and some of the drivers had turned on their headlights. Everyone and everything looked normal, as if there was no great upheaval and nothing in the world had been disturbed.

Twenty-Two

I DIDN'T TRY CALLING GLORIA AGAIN. Instead, I hoped to see her in school and talk with her directly. On Monday I caught her between first and second hour classes, but as soon as I approached she turned and walked in the opposite direction. My next chance to speak with her came when she left school for lunch. I ran after her as she walked down Cedar Avenue alone. She turned and looked at me as I caught up with her. Her face was contorted with hurt and anger no less intense than the afternoon I had driven to her house. "Just leave me alone," she said, her face flushed and her voice high and tense.

"Gloria, please. Give me a chance to explain. I don't know what all you've heard, but nothing happened."

"Just leave me alone," she repeated.

I could see a film of tears in her eyes. The depth of her emotion was frightening to me, as if it sprang from some abyss of pain beyond my comprehension. I watched as the tears spilled onto her cheeks, her dark eyes both defiant and full of sorrow. I stood and watched her as she turned and walked away. I wanted to run after her, grab her by the shoulders and somehow make her understand, but I was paralyzed by her anger. I believed that anything I might do at that moment would only make matters irretrievably worse.

What had happened with Gloria eclipsed my concerns about how I should deal with Tom. I simply talked with him as if nothing had occurred between us, and made no reference to my attempt to avoid him. I gave him no explanation and no apology. And he said nothing about it either. I thought at first there might be some residual anger or unspoken tension between us, but whatever I may have sensed or imagined quickly faded away. I told him Gloria had heard about the night we had taken the O'Hara twins to Lake Nokomis, and how hurt and angry she was.

"Jean was probably shooting her mouth off," Tom said as we sat in Lida's. He took a long drag on his cigarette. "Just explain what happened and tell her you're sorry. Girls love it when you say you're sorry. It makes them feel like they're running the show."

"You don't get it, Tom. She won't even speak to me. And her mom isn't too crazy about me at the moment, either." I wanted him to understand fully how upset I was about what had happened, and that the situation was not something that could be easily solved or cavalierly dismissed.

Tom took another drag on his cigarette. He squinted one eye as smoke curled back toward his face. The jukebox began to play "A Fool Such As I." We both fell silent as Elvis Presley began to sing the lament for a lost love. "Hey, Will, maybe that's your new theme song."

"Damn it, Tom, it isn't funny. I don't know if she's ever going to talk with me again. Not everything is a goddamned joke, you know."

"Hey, take it easy, Will. It isn't the end of the world."

I searched my shirt pocket for a cigarette and matches, but came up empty.

Tom pulled out his pack of Luckies. "Here, have one of mine," he said and snapped the pack against his other hand, expertly shaking a wedge of several cigarettes loose.

"Thanks," I said after a moment. "Sorry. I didn't mean to sound so pissed, but I really can't seem to get through to her."

Tom handed me his lighter. "She'll come around. Just give it some time."

I lit my cigarette and handed the lighter back to Tom. "And what if she doesn't, Tom? What if she decides that no matter what I have to say, she just doesn't trust me anymore?"

"You want to know what I really think?"

"Yeah, I do." I wanted to add that I was especially interested in hearing how he thought this could be straightened out, since he was the one who had advised me not to say anything to her in the first place, but I realized that was unfair and didn't say anything further.

"If she won't even give you a chance to explain, then maybe she isn't as wonderful as you think." He didn't say any more, but watched me closely, as if he were waiting to see how I would react. "We're all strange people deep down inside, Will. Remember Cindy, and how nuts I was about her? Turned out she wasn't who I thought she was at all." He waited a heartbeat or two. "Gloria might not be exactly who you thinks she is."

"Maybe, but it's complicated. She's had lots of disappointments, and this really hurt her . . ." What Tom had said made me feel uncertain about Gloria for the first time. I found something undeniable about his logic.

"Like I say, give it some time," he said more sympathetically. "If she's who you think she is, she'll come around. And if she doesn't, there are plenty of other girls in the world."

"Yeah, right," I said. I tried not to give any hint that his advice had shaken me and made me more confused than ever about my own feelings.

Tom reached across the table and punched my left shoulder. "Now don't start worrying on me, Will. Hell, old Jean O'Hara will still go out with you—and she knows how to keep the boys happy."

"Yeah, right," I said. I looked out into the blue-gray haze of the smoke-filled cafe. Something by Fats Domino came on the jukebox, the distinctive shuffle beat pounding hard in my chest.

* * * * *

THAT AFTERNOON WE HAD AN ALL-SCHOOL ASSEMBLY in the auditorium. A speaker from the Quaker Oats Company was giving a speech on liberty. The name of the speech was "Let Freedom Ring." When I got to my seat, I scanned the crowd for Gloria, but couldn't find her anywhere in the milling, noisy throng of students that streamed into the auditorium and cascaded down into the seats on the main floor and in the balcony. I stood and watched the area on the ground floor where I knew she usually sat, but couldn't find her in the crowd. The principal was already at the podium urging students to take their seats and quiet down when I heard someone across the aisle call out to me. It was my restaurant co-worker, Bill Freeman.

"You working tonight, Will?"

"Yeah, yeah, I'm working," I shouted back, angry that he had interrupted my search.

"Okay, I'll see you there," he said, a generous smile unfazed by my angry reply.

"Yeah, okay," I said, and forced myself to be pleasant. "I'll see you at work, Bill." With that I took my seat. The principal was already in mid-introduction and the auditorium had grown quiet, except for scattered coughing and the creak of wooden seats as a thousand students settled in for the speech.

The guest speaker was dressed in a Quaker costume like the one worn by the character on the cereal box, except that his hat and coat were a pale gray instead of the customary jet black ensemble. He wore a white wig that flared out under either side of his broad-brimmed hat. The wig glistened in the spotlight as he approached the podium. As he began to speak, I slumped down in my seat in the darkened auditorium and folded my arms across my chest. I leaned back, let my head drop forward and closed my eyes. I heard only the droning, meaningless sound of his voice and sporadic coughing in the audience, lost now in my own thoughts. I must have dozed off for a time, because it seemed only a matter of minutes later that I was startled by thunderous applause and the muffled roar of the student body rising up out of their seats and heading for the exits.

As I neared one of the doors, I spotted a red ponytail bobbing a short distance in front of me. "Jean? Jean O'Hara, is that you?"

Jean turned to look back at me, lost her balance and was nearly knocked to the floor by the stream of students who rushed around her. "Hey, stranger," she called out. Her faced brightened when she saw me.

"I need to talk with you," I said and pointed to the hallway on our right.

Jean stepped into the side hallway and waited for me by one of the narrow lockers. She leaned back against the locker and cradled an armful of books against her chest. "Hey, Will, long time, no see. How have you been?" She was chewing gum and the rate of mastication had increased with her apparent excitement.

She was so pleasant and clearly happy to see me that it took a conscious effort on my part to not respond in kind. "Look, Jean, did you tell Gloria Jensen about the night we went out to Lake Nokomis?"

The smile vanished from her face and she stopped chewing her gum. "What? No, I never said anything to her about it."

"Well, she heard about it somewhere. I don't know exactly what all she heard, but now she won't have anything to do with me—won't even talk to me." I could feel my anger build as I spoke about it. Jean pressed her books more tightly to her body, as if she needed them for protection.

"I don't think I've ever talked to Gloria at all," she said, her voice now devoid of all joy and her eyes wide with apprehension.

"Then how the hell did she hear about it?" The more timid she became, the more my frustration and anger increased. I didn't understand why I was becoming so incensed, but I was aware that I was losing control.

Jean was silent. There was a sudden redness in her cheeks and her eyes grew watery. "I told one of my girlfriends about it," She said at last. "Maybe she said something and it got back to Gloria, I don't know." She didn't say any more, but looked steadily at me as her lower lip trembled slightly.

"And what exactly did you tell your friend? What did you tell her?" The second time I asked my question, it came out so loudly that several students turned and looked at us. I looked back at one of the students who were staring at us. He stopped watching and continued on down the hallway.

"I told her everything about that night." Jean had now lost her timidity, finding her practiced toughness that she no doubt had needed all her life. "I told her the truth."

"And what was that?"

Jean stuck her chin out defiantly and leaned toward me. Her words spilled out rapidly. "I told her that I tried to get you to go for a skinny dip, but you wouldn't do it. I told her Tom had set the whole thing up and you were all nervous about being out with another girl when it was really Gloria you liked. I told her I thought you were cute and funny and a really nice guy—and that I hoped I'd maybe see you again sometime."

"That's all? You didn't say anything more? You didn't make anything up?"

She leaned back against the locker, her eyes once again glistening with tears. "No, Will, I didn't tell her anything more. And I don't need to make anything up, 'cause I'm sure some of the sweet little things around school have me fucking your brains out in the stories they pass along. I know how they talk about me and my sister behind our backs. I don't care about any of them. But don't worry. You'll be okay, Will. Guys don't have to worry about that kind of stuff at all."

"Look, Jean . . ." I groped for the right words. I believed everything she had said, and already regretted my verbal assault. "Look . . . I think you're really a decent girl and I'm sorry I got so mad—"

"Forget it," she said, talking over my apology. She held her books tightly and looked down at the floor. She sniffed twice and didn't look up.

The warning bell rang. I knew I would be late for class, but I couldn't leave her like that. I heard the sound of distant footsteps fade into silence. I looked up and down the now deserted hallway and saw the last two open classroom doors swing shut. "Jean, I'm really sorry, I mean it. It's just that I've been going crazy trying to explain to Gloria that nothing happened, but she won't even talk to me." I reached out to touch her shoulder, but she pulled away.

"Just go," she said without looking up. And then, "You're going to be late for class."

"I'm really sorry, Jean."

"It's okay. Just go."

"I don't want to leave you like this."

She still wouldn't look at me. "I'll be all right, just go."

I started down the silent hall, with Jean still leaning against the locker. I had only gone a few steps when she called out to me. She looked up from where she was standing, her cheeks now wet with tears. "I was real proud that I got to go out with a guy like you. I mean, I know it wasn't really a date or anything, but I was real proud anyway."

Twenty-Three

I FELT MISERABLE ABOUT EVERYTHING. In the deep silence of the autumn nights, as I tried to go to sleep, I couldn't banish thoughts of Gloria and Tom and Jean from my mind. I didn't think my transgressions had been so serious, yet the consequences left me feeling ashamed and nearly friendless. I should have told Gloria immediately about that night at Nokomis, as I had intended. I should not have angrily confronted Jean, or accused her of lying about what had happened between us. Tom also seeped into these late night thoughts of guilt and regret. I should never have lied about my plans for the evening and whether or not I could spend some time with him. And then my thoughts would spiral further into a world of doubt and troubling possibilities.

Maybe Tom was right about Gloria. It was possible I really didn't know or understand her as well as I thought. After all, wouldn't any reasonable person at least give me some opportunity to explain? Perhaps, as Tom said, we were all strange people deep inside—stranger than we cared to admit to ourselves or anyone else. On the other hand, Tom didn't know about Martin and the things Gloria had lived with and seen, and how that had tempered her view of the world. And Jean was really no different than anyone else, and hadn't deserved my anger. In fact, the more I thought about her, the more I thought she was so much better than the crowd who gleefully made her an object of their derision. These thoughts went on and on, tumbling one after the other, leading to more questions without answers and finally to shallow, restive sleep.

It didn't help that we were reading *The Great Gatsby* in Mrs. Bridges's English class. We had finished with the Romantic English poets and were now concentrating on American novelists. Whenever we discussed Jay Gatsby's fevered efforts to regain the love of

Daisy Buchanan, my thoughts would drift to Gloria and her obstinate refusal to speak with me. Someone would read a brief passage from the book and I would be immediately consumed by my own situation, no longer aware of the class discussion. Mrs. Bridges seemed wired to some intricate mechanism that sensed these lapses of concentration in her students, and her immediate response was to bring the wayward student back into the academic orbit with a direct question.

"Will, what do you think about that?"

I looked up at Mrs. Bridges, who stood in front of me in the aisle. I glanced at Junior, who had turned around and was trying to mouth words that would give me some hint about the discussion. "I . . . I'm sorry," I said. "I guess I lost track of which passage we were on."

Mrs. Bridges paused for a slightly punitive moment, and then helped me back into the discussion. "We were discussing the passage in chapter six, when Nick tells Gatsby not to expect too much of Daisy, because, as Nick tells him, you can't repeat the past."

"Oh, yes," I said, and searched frantically for the passage.

"How does Gatsby respond? And what do you think his response tells us about him?"

I found the passage. "Well, Gatsby says that of course you can repeat the past. And he says he's going to make everything just as it was before he lost her—Daisy."

"Yes, that's right." Mrs. Bridges turned away, walked down the aisle and sat at her desk. It wasn't until she was seated that she spoke again. She looked directly at me, a gentle, forgiving smile on her face. "And what do you think that tells us about Gatsby, Will?"

In silence, I read the passage again. I looked up at Mrs. Bridges and at the large, round wall clock above her head that ticked away each minute of the morning. I felt little streams of perspiration run from underneath my arms as Mrs. Bridges waited silently for an answer. "Well, I guess it's like Nick says at the beginning of the novel, that Gatsby is romantic and full of hope." I heard two or more girls giggle inexplicably at what I'd said, which made me certain that Mrs. Bridges was looking for a more insightful and sophisticated answer, but my thoughts were divided between the story and my own questions about reconciling with Gloria.

"Yes, good point, Will. You're right. This is the unfailingly romantic Gatsby who Nick talks about at the start of the novel. Thank you, Will." Mrs. Bridges glanced around the room. "And would anyone else like to comment on Gatsby's belief that we can repeat the past? Was he wrong? What made him think such a thing might be possible?"

The room was silent, with only three or four hands raised in the most hesitant and tentative manner. I felt some small comfort in the fact that so few were willing to respond. Mrs. Bridges called on Sandra Hart, or "Sandy Hart the smart fart," as she was known by nearly the entire junior class. "Yes, Sandra, what do you think of Gatsby's faith in repeating the past?"

"Well," Sandy said. She drew the word out so that it sounded like "w-u-u-l-l-l," her standard introduction to what was certain to be a prolonged but incredibly erudite response. "I agree with Will," she said and shook her long, blonde hair back, her face raised at an angle toward Mrs. Bridges. "This is the statement of a hopelessly romantic person whom Nick both admires and at the same time disapproves of. And I think his faith in being able to repeat the past is because of his belief that anything is possible and anything can be gained with money and power—as if he could win Daisy's love back with a display of his wealth, just as he believed he could buy respectability. I actually believe that F. Scott Fitzgerald, through this character, was describing America in the nineteen-twenties, when America was engaged in a sort of irresponsible and unrealistic post-war party. Of course, the party ended tragically with the Great Depression."

I was glad that Sandy had said she agreed with me. Most of the remainder of what she had said seemed like showing off to me, but was probably the sort of answer Mrs. Bridges had hoped I would give.

"Very good, Sandra."

"Thank you, Mrs. Bridges."

"Sandra makes a very interesting point in tying the character of Gatsby to the times in which he lived," Mrs. Bridges began, "and pointing out that we might even see him as representing that period. That was a very fine observation. America was, in a sense, having one great party in what are now called the 'Roaring Twenties,' and maybe anything did seem possible at the time. But I also wonder if America has really changed all that much in terms of thinking that money can solve all problems. Was that something we believed only in the twenties, or do we still believe it today?"

Jim Zena flashed across my mind as I listened to what Mrs. Bridges said. A moment or two passed, and then I began to think of Gloria again. I wondered if I was as hopeless and doomed as Gatsby in thinking I could make everything right again. I thought of the upcoming Thanksgiving holiday and the fact that Dee would be coming home for nearly a week. I looked forward to seeing Dee and seeking her advice, if everything was still a mess by the time we were on break. I couldn't help but wonder if, as Gatsby believed, I could not only win my girl back but also erase all memory and emotion of what had come between us. Or would my failure to disclose what had happened leave a residue of anger and mistrust that could never be completely undone? Even if the memory faded, would the feeling remain? I knew it was silly and expansive to compare myself to Gatsby, and yet I did feel a sort of kinship to him and his fictional plight. And then I saw Mrs. Bridges peer at me over her glasses, her eyes betraying her disappointment at my inattention.

"We'll be finishing *The Great Gatsby* next week," she said to the class, her eyes still fixed on me. "I would like you all to think about the character of Tom Buchanan as we conclude this novel. I would like you to think about how society might judge Tom, and, in contrast, how society might judge Jay Gatsby. We'll read in class from chapter seven tomorrow, and let's plan to finish the book one week from today." The bell rang as she concluded her instructions. "See you all tomorrow."

Mrs. Bridges stood by the door as the class filed out, nodding to some students and saying goodbye to others. I sensed she was going to stop me—and I was right. She touched my left forearm just as I was about to leave the room. "Will," she said, a look of sincere concern on her face, "is everything okay? You seem to be having a great deal of difficulty concentrating in class lately." She spoke in a hushed, confidential tone.

"No, it's nothing, really, just stuff," I said. What else could I say? Mrs. Bridges was clearly not content with my answer, but I was fairly certain that if I could avoid her questions until the warning bell she wouldn't delay me further. We stood and stared at each other for several seconds, until I broke off eye contact and looked at the floor.

She took hold of my left forearm and shook it twice. A slender, gold bracelet swayed in response on her fragile wrist. "You know, Will, you could be a very fine student if you wanted to be. You could be one of my top students. If something is troubling you and keeping you from concentrating, I'd like to help."

I didn't say anything. After all, she hadn't asked me a question.

And then it came. "Is there anything I might do to help?"

I looked at her. It made me a little sad to see how truly concerned she was, and to know that there was nothing she could possibly do to help. "It's just some stuff at work," I said. "I've been having some problems with my boss, but I think things are going to be okay from now on." I thought that sounded pretty legitimate and definitely beyond her realm of authority.

She looked directly at me, apparently searching my face for some telltale sign that I might be less than completely honest. "All right," she said at last. "Well, you'd better get along to your next class. Remember, Will, the most important thing you can do at your age is to be a good student and learn all you can. That should be your first concern."

"Okay. Well, thanks a lot, Mrs. Bridges. Really, thanks for asking. I'll try and get on top of this stuff." She let go of my arm and I hurried down the hall, absolutely convinced that she knew I had lied to her.

Twenty-Four

IF GLORIA WOULDN'T TALK TO ME, I thought I might write a letter to her that explained everything. It seemed a desperate and even melodramatic action to take—the sort of thing I would never mention to Tom—but it also appeared to be the only realistic choice left open to me. And so I began to compose the letter in my mind at work one evening, making special note of how I would explain I had initially intended to tell her all about the night at Nokomis, but as time passed it seemed so trivial and inconsequential that it was hardly worth mentioning. In fact, I would point out, I had nearly forgotten about it entirely. That would need to be artfully crafted and not sound contrived or exaggerated. The exact wording would have to be carefully worked out on paper. I would also explain that, in retrospect, I realized my mistake and understood why she had reacted so strongly to what looked like deception on my part. Was this taking on too much blame? Was Tom right about girls wanting an apology so that they felt they were in control? I began to compose again, backing off the apology to some degree. I tweaked and polished what would be in the letter, and even began to try some of the sentences out loud, whispering to myself. The mental editing was interrupted as Bill Freeman leaned into the serving window.

"Hey, Will, I need two South Minneapolis specials." He looked back and forth, scanning the length of the kitchen. More quietly, he asked, "Is Jim still here?"

I pulled two hamburger patties from the meat drawer and threw them on the grill. "Yeah, I guess he's working late tonight. I don't know why."

Bill stared through the thick lenses of his glasses, his paper hat pulled low on his forehead. "Okay," he said, sounding as if he were in a position to approve or disapprove Jim's hours. "We've been getting along pretty well, anyway," he added.

"Yeah, that's good."

I began to edit my letter again as I watched the burgers fry. Within a minute or two the burgers had thickened and grown less pink around the edge, but my letter hadn't progressed at all. I threw two strips of bacon on the grill and set the metal press on top of them as I flipped the burgers. I hated all the psychological machinations I was going through with my letter idea. Why couldn't Gloria just listen to what had happened? Why did this need to get all tangled up with who was in control and what hurts other people may have inflicted in the past? And then I saw Jim tying on his apron and walking toward me through the galley.

"Matt called in sick this afternoon, so I'll stay as long as two of us are needed for the supper hour," he said as he approached.

"Great. Thanks, Jim," I said. There was unusual buoyancy to his walk, a certain lightness in his demeanor I had never seen before. He grabbed hold of one of the large fryer baskets, as if he needed something as a counter-weight to keep him from floating up to the ceiling.

"Been getting many orders?" he asked as he shook the basket.

"No. It's been pretty slow."

My news didn't seem to dampen his spirits at all. "Yeah, that's all right. We'll maybe just see a small rush tonight. After all, it's midweek." He gave the basket a second shake and hooked it back on the fryer. He stepped up to the steam table and began checking all the inserts as I put cheese slices on top of the two burgers.

Jim closed the last section of the steam table. He began to walk toward the grill, singing as he approached. "Nine more months and ten more days I'll be out of the calaboose. Nine more months and ten more days they're gonna turn me loose."

I picked the bacon up off the grill with tongs and placed the strips on top of the melting cheese. I tossed chopped onions on the grill, stirred them with my spatula and inhaled the rich aroma as they turned from white to golden brown. "Well, you're feeling great," I said as he repeated his lyrics about getting out of the calaboose.

He stopped singing. "Yeah, yeah. Why not?" he said.

Bill came around the corner just as I was about put to up his order. "You're right on time, Bill. I'm just finishing these."

Bill stopped at the window, all hat and glasses as he stared nervously between Jim and me and said nothing.

"Hello there, Bill," Jim said and then broke into another chorus of his song. He closed his eyes and raised his face toward the ceiling as his song rose an octave.

"Hi, Jim," Bill said haltingly as he picked the two plates up off the counter. He looked at me and made a quizzical V-shape with his eyebrows. I smiled back at Bill and gave him an "it beats me" shrug of my shoulders.

Jim finished up his song and leaned back against the ledge of the steam table. "Did I ever tell you I was in the movies?" He grinned and waited for me to respond as I scraped the grill clean with my spatula.

"You were in the movies? No kidding?"

"Yes, sir. Hard to believe, isn't it?"

This seemed like a tricky conversational query, and I didn't want to say anything to spoil his ebullient mood. "So, what happened?" I asked. That seemed to strike a diplomatic tone of interest without any implied judgment as to his worthiness to be in a movie.

"Well, sir, it was when I was in the Army. I was stationed out in California for a while and some of these Hollywood types were making a war film near the base. Anyway, they needed a bunch of soldiers for a scene where they were loading men onto a troop ship." He laughed and shook his head, evidently recalling some particularly amusing aspect of the memory. "Damnedest thing you ever saw. They had this big . . . I don't know . . . kind of a screen-type thing that looked like the side of a ship. It was kind of a big, flat wall painted to look like a ship. Then they had about twenty or thirty of us walking up this gangplank into the ship. But when we got to the other side, we just walked down some steps and around to the front again. So you had these twenty or thirty guys going round and round in circles—up into the ship, around to the front, and then back in line to walk into the ship again. Of course, it looked like hundreds of us."

"Huh."

"We must have gone around in that circle fifty times. It was the damnedest thing you ever saw."

Two order slips had been dropped at the serving window. I picked them up while Jim continued with his story. "These are both dinner orders," I said and handed them to Jim. He took them from me. He didn't bother to look at them, but simply placed them on the counter in front of himself.

"Here we were, full duffel bags, rifles and everything, just like we were shipping out, but going round and round in circles. And then this one little guy—real loud—I guess he was the director or something—he kept making them film the scene over and over. I can still see him, black hair all slicked back and running all over the place yelling. I thought he was going to have a stroke. So, there we'd go again, walking around in circles and the little guy running all over the place yelling at everybody. Damnedest thing you ever saw."

"Did you get paid for the work?"

"Hah! Are you kidding? It was the Army. Maybe the Army got some money, but none of us saw a damned thing."

"Still, kind of a fun experience, I suppose."

"Yeah," he said and fell silent. He seemed lost in some distant, private moment. "It's funny about stuff like that."

"What do you mean?"

"Well, you know, the closer you get to some things the more disappointed you are."

I finished scraping the grill and put the spatula back on the shelf just above it. I turned toward Jim, his mood now less sanguine than it had been just a moment earlier. "I guess I'm not sure what you mean."

"Aw, you know," he said somewhat gruffly, as if I were not the brightest of students. "The closer you get to the heart of some things, the more you see the flaws—like the movies. If you see how they're made, it kind of spoils it for you. I mean, you see how kind of phony everything is."

"Oh, sure," I said, hoping to renew his faith in my intelligence. "I see what you mean."

Jim turned and picked up the two orders he had been ignoring. He read them quickly, slid open two covers on the steam table and began to dish up the dinner orders. "Yeah, it's funny," he said, his mood clearly becoming more sober and reflective, "there's lots of things in life that don't hold up well to close examination. Once you see what things are really like, they kind of lose their attraction."

I assumed that he was about to launch into one of his lectures on "the old bucks" and how only money truly mattered in life, when he once again defied my anticipation of his logic and sentiment.

He put the two orders up on the ledge of the order window, stuck his head into the window and shouted, "Pick up!" Then he turned back to me. He leaned against the ledge of the steam table, removed his chef's hat and wiped his brow with his right sleeve. He put his hat back on and folded his arms across his chest. "Yes, sir, I've seen plenty of things in life that disappointed me—people, religion, politics. Plenty. And just a few things that turned out to be anywhere near what they should have been. And maybe only one or two that were . . . I don't know . . . one or two that pretty much made everything worth it, if you know what I mean."

"I guess," I said, though his specific meaning was lost for me among his abstractions. I didn't say any more. I was beginning to grow uncomfortable with the silence and his steady gaze. Three orders were dropped at the window, on Jim's side, but he ignored them.

"Yeah, the older I get the more I realize there are just a few things in life that make it worth putting up with all the crap."

"Oh," I said, and waited for a lecture on the god of money, but it didn't come.

Jim turned back toward the counter and picked up the order slips. Without comment, he began to dish up the dinners. "Bea and I never had any kids—I told you that. We decided that's how it would be—the two of us. We just couldn't see bringing kids into this world. Just couldn't see it. I don't know, I've second-guessed myself on that one a number of times. Funny, you make all these decisions as a young man that you have to live with as an old man.

The kid makes the choices for the man." He grew silent again as he finished putting the orders together and setting the plates on the window ledge. "Anyway, it doesn't matter now. It's too late to do anything about that, even if the decision we made was a bad one. Those years are gone. No kids for us, not ever. No miracle is going to change that. Done deal."

"Well . . ."

"Pick up," Jim shouted through the window, then turned toward me. "Yeah, so you live with those decisions. And I'm okay with that. Still, you can't help but wonder sometimes about how things might have been. You know?"

"Sure," I said.

Jim turned away from me and leaned his elbows against the serving window. He looked out into the dining room as he continued to talk. "Bea and I have been married for forty-two years now, yet in some ways it seems like only yesterday we were getting hitched." He paused for a moment, and then added dreamily, "You should have seen her when she was young. God, she was beautiful." He looked down at the counter and shook his head, as if he couldn't believe it had all happened so long ago. "Yeah, forty-two years."

"That's a long time," I commented.

Jim's head bobbed and his shoulders shook slightly as he chuckled at my comment. "Yes, sir. But my point is this—it's the best part of my life. The best thing I ever did was marry that woman. And don't get me wrong, we've had plenty of disagreements and times when we wanted to walk out the door—one or the other or both of us. I'm not saying it was all easy. But, I am saying that it's the best thing in life." He turned and looked at me over his shoulder. "That's the whole thing really, finding that one person you can share this crazy life with. That's all I really know for sure. I guess that may sound like a lot of hooey to you—crazy talk from an old man."

"It doesn't sound crazy to me at all," I said. "It makes a lot of sense to me, to tell you the truth." I thought about my letter to Gloria and how badly I wanted at that moment to sit down and begin to put it on paper.

Jim pulled back from the counter and faced me. "Listen, it looks like it's going to be pretty slow tonight. I'm going to go have a cigarette break. If you start getting swamped with orders, just give me a holler."

"Okay, Jim. I should be fine for a while."

"Okay, then," he said and began to walk away as he broke into another chorus of his song about getting out of the calaboose.

Twenty-Five

On Tuesday in the week before Thanksgiving, the weather turned painfully cold. The early, slight covering of snow had been lost in the warmth of the following days, leaving no trace behind. But dry and bitter winds from the north brought temperatures that dipped below the zero mark, hardened the moistened ground and left no illusions about what was to come. As I crossed Cedar Avenue without jacket or hat, the wind swept along the cavernous street, passed unabated through the leafless trees, and stung my eyes, ears, and fingertips. In my rush to get inside, I pulled too quickly on the door to Lida's, causing the knob to slip from my hand and the door to bang shut. I grasped the knob more tightly, swung the door open and burst into the café both physically and verbally. "Shit, it's cold out there."

Tom looked out from under a curlicue of smoke. He blew two smoke rings, laughed and shook his head. "It's only going to get worse, Will. You might as well get used to it."

He was sitting in a booth near the door. I dropped into the seat across from him. I rubbed my hands together. "Shit, Tom, this is brutal. It's too early to be this cold."

Tom mashed out his cigarette. He pushed aside a plate with a C-shaped smear of ketchup and a few French fries scattered around the edge. "You getting something to eat?"

"Yeah, I'm starved."

The jukebox was playing a Perry Como tune, "Catch a Falling Star," unusually sedate for Lida's. There were fewer customers than usual during the lunch hour, and the standard fog of cigarette smoke was less dense than normal. The sparse gathering was probably due to the cold, I thought fleetingly. I picked up a menu and stared at it blankly, already knowing what I would order.

"You working tonight?" Tom said.

"No," I said absently. Lida approached and waited for me to put the menu down. She said nothing as she took my order for a burger, fries and a Coke.

"You want to do something tonight?"

"Like what?"

"I don't know . . . start a rock and roll band? Stick up a bank?"

"Funny, Tom. Look out, Milton Berle," I said. "To tell you the truth, I've got a writing assignment I need to finish, and this is about the only night I have to do it." I was thinking of my letter to Gloria. It was my own assignment to myself, but it wasn't a lie—I did plan to get the letter done that evening.

"How about we just cruise around for an hour or so after school?"

"Naw, I really don't think so, Tom. Not tonight."

"C'mon, Will, don't be such a pussy. You're going to kill yourself with boredom."

I lit a cigarette and waved out the match. "What's the big deal, Tom? It's Tuesday night. Why do we have to go out tonight?"

Tom looked at the door as two girls rushed into to the café, laughing and holding themselves tightly about their midsections, cheeks and noses pink from the frigid air. "Yeah, it's nothing. Forget it," he said, his voice sounding resigned and disappointed.

"Seriously, what's the deal?"

"Nothing. I just don't want sit around the damned house all night, okay? The place is more depressing than school."

"Is your old man drinking again?" I said without thinking, and regretted immediately that I had raised such a sensitive issue. "Sorry, Tom."

He gave no indication that he was bothered by what I'd said. "Not at the moment, but the holidays are coming up. That's always a great time to get loaded. You've never really experienced Christmas until you've experienced a drunken Christmas."

"Smoke Gets in Your Eyes" by The Platters began to play on the jukebox, selected by the two girls who had just breezed into the café. They laughed and ducked into one of the booths near us as the music came on.

Lida arrived with my order, collected my money and left again, all without speaking. As I stubbed out my cigarette and began to eat, Tom leaned forward. "So, have you gotten everything patched up with Gloria?"

His question sounded perfunctory to me, as if he were asking me what time it was or if it had begun to snow. "Not yet." I bit into my burger. I assumed he really didn't want to hear anything further about it.

"Yeah?" he said pensively. "That's too bad."

I looked up at him. He appeared to be serious, without the usual caustic remark hovering in wait. "Yeah, well, I'm still trying to get her to listen to me."

"You're really nuts about her, aren't you?"

I waited a moment or two, still unsure whether or not I was being set up for a joke. "Yeah, I am," I said at last.

"I never meant to mess things up for you. I didn't think our little night at the beach was that big a deal," Tom said. "I just want you to know that."

I was stunned. This wasn't the tough, disdainful person I knew. "I know that, Tom, really. It's okay."

One of the two girls who had selected the song by The Platters poked her head around the corner of the booth. "Hey, one of you guys got a light?" she asked and held an unlit cigarette out between her index and middle fingers, as if she needed to demonstrate that she did, indeed, have need for a light.

"Sure," Tom said, his voice full of impatience.

The lightless girl got up, exited her booth and stood before Tom. She was short and stocky, with dark hair and wide-set pale blue eyes that darted back and forth as they searched Tom's face. She was wearing a bright skirt of red-and-blue plaid and a tight black sweater that buttoned up the front. The top three buttons, I noticed, were undone. She bent forward from the waist, her rump thrust generously in the air and whatever cleavage she enjoyed aimed directly at Tom's face. She watched him closely as he snapped open his lighter and held it out for her. She took hold of his hand and held the lighter in place as she dragged on the cigarette. Once it was lit, she stood up and held it high and away from her face, her fingers pointed toward the ceiling, her elbow tucked in against her waist. "Thanks. Hey, ain't you Tom McCarthy?"

"Yes."

"You know my sister Jenny—Jenny Dieter?"

"I don't think so."

"She's a junior, like you. I'm Karen. Me and Sue are sophomores," she said, evidently referring to her unseen boothmate.

"Okay, Karen. I think I'll do you a favor. If I meet your sister, I won't tell her I saw you smoking." The two stared at each other, Karen Dieter seemingly unable to fathom Tom's intent. "Goodbye, Karen," he said.

After an instant of delayed comprehension, Karen Dieter's face lost all expression. She spoke just one word before she left: "Dink."

Tom turned back to me. "Anyway," he said, as if he had just swatted away a fly, "getting back together with her is a really big deal to you, isn't it?"

"Yeah, it is," I said cautiously.

"I like girls as much as any guy, but I guess I've never felt that way about one. You know what I mean?" He seemed bewildered and lacking any reference point that might help him understand my devotion to Gloria.

"Yeah, I know what you mean. I guess I never felt this way before either. I don't even know if I can explain it. I mean, it started out I just liked her because she's so damned cute, but as I got to know her it all got more complicated. She's smart and funny and really means what she says. There's nothing phony about her. Her dad died when she was just a baby and she's had to put up with a lot of crap at home. She hasn't had it all that easy." I stopped there. I felt it would betray a trust to tell Tom about Gloria's stepfather and the secrets she had confided. "I don't know, Tom, I just need to make it right with her again." I wanted to tell him I loved her, but I couldn't do it. I couldn't say that out loud to Tom, not yet.

Tom sat back in the booth and took a pack of Lucky Strikes from his breast pocket. He extracted a cigarette from the pack and began to tap it against his lighter, packing the tobacco down tightly. He looked at the cigarette as he continued to tap it over and over against the silver Zippo. "Yeah, that's cool, Will," he said without looking up. "You just might be the luckiest guy I know," he said. He snorted a little laugh and shook his head. It was not a laugh of contempt or ridicule, but a laugh of unveiled envy. He lit the cigarette, took a long drag and exhaled slowly. "Yeah, you're a lucky son of a bitch, Will."

* * * * *

Just a few hours later on that snowless and bitterly cold autumn afternoon, life was unalterably changed. Tom was driving west on Twenty-sixth Street toward Bloomington Avenue, alone, seeking out some small escape from hostility or boredom or whatever mundane frustrations must have felt intolerable to him at the moment. Headed north along one of the intersecting streets was a seventy-two-year-old man with no history that could have foretold what was about to happen. As the older man approached the stop sign at Twenty-sixth Street, he experienced a violent and unprecedented neurologic storm—a chaotic firing of synapses and wild cerebral electrical activity that caused him to lose control of his limbs, and in that same moment, consciousness. His right foot thrust forward and pinned the gas pedal to the floor as the seizure stripped him of any awareness or willful response.

By the time his car reached the intersection, it was racing at more than fifty miles per hour. In an instant of random, tragic synchronicity, his car slammed into Tom's on the driver's door. The explosion of metal and shattering glass could be felt and heard over two city blocks. Tom's car was catapulted onto the northwest corner of the streets. The force of the collision was so great that it ripped all four tires completely away from their rims. His door was crushed shut and there were pools of antifreeze and oil and blood draining onto the sidewalk and frozen boulevard. The older man's car was just below Tom's, angled slightly toward the west, its hood crumpled and tented, the windshield shattered into a thousand tiny webs. The horn of the old man's car wailed incessantly, like the plaintive cry of a gravely wounded beast.

The nearby houses emptied out as the occupants ran down embankments and over neighbors' hardened lawns and through shrubs in their rush to reach the accident. People walking in the area hurried toward the site, and cars slowed and stopped as drivers gawked at the wreckage. People gathered near the cars in a thickening circle of humanity, shocked and uncertain and shouting to one another what needed to be done. Some in the crowd attempted to remove the old man from his car even while he continued to seizure, but were successfully discouraged by others in the growing throng. In less than five minutes, two police squads and an ambulance arrived.

The older man regained consciousness by the time the ambulance attendants reached him. He appeared to have survived the wreck with only cuts and bruises, as they hurried him by stretcher to the ambulance.

The younger driver was already lost.

Twenty-Six

THE VISITATION FOR TOM wasn't held until Friday evening. The room in the white-brick funeral chapel on Chicago Avenue was small and warm and redolent of flowers. The casket was closed, with a picture of Tom sitting atop the highly polished mahogany lid. The photo was old, taken at the time of his eighth grade graduation from Holy Rosary School. In the photo, Tom was wearing a light gray suit coat, white shirt and maroon tie, smiling only slightly and looking away from the camera, off into the distance. The thin line of his lips, turned up just perceptibly at the corners, conveyed some unknown mischievous thought that would remain forever hidden.

My parents and I had driven separately, and I stayed on after they left for home. It was all beyond belief and comprehension, beyond any logic or meaning. In some strange, unarticulated way, I felt that if I stayed there long enough I might begin to make some sense of it all.

The crowd had been small at first and then grew until the parlor was uncomfortably stretched beyond capacity. Despite the number of people, the room remained unusually quiet. The murmur of voices was a steady hum, broken by an occasional burst of laughter or the sound of Tom's mother or sister crying. The family remained huddled near one another in the middle of the room. His younger brother and sister stood together, just a foot or two away from their parents. Tom's father wore an ill-fitting brown suit that was long out of style and shiny in the elbows and knees. More than uncomfortable, he looked bewildered and angry. His eyes scanned the crowd, as if he might discover among them the reason or source of this inexplicable pain. Whatever there had been between Tom and his father, his look told me it was something more than just loathing and anger.

I spoke to Tom's brother and sister. I noticed immediately how much they had grown since I'd last seen them, which had perhaps been as much as six months earlier. I tried to remember their ages. Dan was now thirteen and Catherine was eleven, I recalled. Dan's eyes were red, but he was holding back the tears. *A tough guy,* I thought, *just like his big brother.* He wore slacks, a white shirt and black tie but no coat. He looked so much like Tom that for a moment I couldn't speak. Catherine was wearing a long, dark blue dress. She had tears in her eyes and hugged me around the waist when I told them both how sorry I was. They tried hard to maintain what they must have determined was proper behavior. They both thanked me for coming and Dan even shook my hand very formally before I turned to their parents.

Mr. McCarthy saw me first and nodded his head in recognition but said nothing. A moment later, Mrs. McCarthy turned away from a woman who had been speaking to her and holding both her hands. When she looked at me her eyes instantly welled up with tears and she threw her arms around me. She held me so tightly and I was so close to tears myself, I could scarcely breathe. "I'm so sorry, Mrs. McCarthy," was all I managed to get out.

"My baby is gone, Will. My baby is gone." She held on tight as she repeated those few words over and over.

"I know. I'm so sorry," I said. My throat was constricted and numb with sorrow and I couldn't say anything more—nor did I really know what more there was that I could say. When she finally released me, I stood back and held her hands and repeated my only thought once more. A gray-haired woman approached and drew Mrs. McCarthy's attention away from me.

I turned to Mr. McCarthy. To my surprise, he reached out to shake my hand. His grip was strong as he leaned forward to whisper to me. "Thanks for coming, Will. You were the best friend Tom ever had. I know that's how he thought of you."

"Thanks so much, Mr. McCarthy. I felt the same about him." I could feel tears gathering in my eyes. "I'm so sorry."

Mr. McCarthy nodded as he continued to shake my hand. "Thanks for coming," he repeated, and it was then I detected the faint smell of whiskey and noted the slight alcoholic glaze to his eyes. He let go of my hand and turned to someone else who was waiting to talk with him. I nodded and moved on through the crowd to a table at a near wall.

A large corkboard sat atop a folding table and leaned up against the wall. It was one of several such boards covered with photos. There were old black-and-white pictures of Tom as a young boy riding his bike, posing with the family at a birthday gathering, smiling broadly next to a scrawny, sparsely decorated Christmas tree and dozens of other pictures to mark moments of his childhood. Tom was older in the next series of photos, and most of these were in color. There was one of Tom and me in our robes at our eighth grade graduation from Holy Rosary, standing in front of the school, smiling triumphantly and holding our diplomas aloft. There was a photo of Tom and members of our Boy Scout Troop, with Tom making rabbit ears behind my head. I studied each photo. Most of them brought back vivid memories, but a scant few I found I couldn't recall, and that bothered me—as if Tom was already fading from memory. It was while I studied one of these mysterious and forgotten photographs that I noticed Coach Phillips just a few feet away.

He was looking at one of the boards with several members of the South High football team gathered around him. I thought he glanced at me for just an instant, but I quickly turned my attention back to the photos in front of me. And then I could hear his voice rise slightly above the steady drone of the crowd. "Yeah, he was one hell of a player," he said. "I'll tell you something about Tom McCarthy, he was no damned quitter. No, sir, that young man had no quit in him."

I felt the coach's remark was unquestionably targeted at me, and my face grew hot with embarrassment and anger. Without any effort of logic, I realized immediately that such an inane and irreverent remark deserved no response, and yet his ridiculous barb was more than I could bear. I couldn't let his ignorant slight go unanswered.

As I turned toward the coach, uncertain what I would say, I saw Junior Kandowski break away from the small gathering of players. "Will," he said and held out his arms and clapped me on both shoulders. "Will, I can't tell you how sorry I am about what happened to Tom. I know you two were close as brothers, and this has got to hurt you as much as anyone."

As he held me by my shoulders, I saw Coach Phillips and the other players turn and walk away. "Thanks, Junior," I said, taking a deep breath. My anger at the coach was now displaced by appreciation for Junior's sympathy. "Yeah, I can't believe it. I just can't believe it. I had lunch with him just a few hours before the accident, and then he was . . . he was . . ." My voice now defied my efforts to control it. It shook and cracked and then deserted me entirely. For a moment, I couldn't speak at all as the senselessness and finality of what had happened became more and more real to me. "He wanted me," I gasped, as I struggled to regain my voice. "He wanted me to go cruising around with him after school. I told him I couldn't, that I had stuff to do."

"I'm sorry, Will," Junior said.

"You know what was one of the last things he ever said to me?"

"No, I don't, Will."

"He said I was a lucky son of a bitch. Think of that." I tried to laugh at the irony of the statement, but lost my voice again in an abortive sob. "God, he was more right than he knew," I choked out.

* * * * *

THE FUNERAL MASS WAS HELD the next morning at Holy Rosary. Both my mother and father had to work and Dee wasn't home on break yet, so I attended the Mass on my own. As I sat in the church and watched the altar boys, I couldn't help but think back to all the funerals and weddings for which Tom and I had served together. The weddings were happy affairs, and there was always an envelope with money for the altar boys following the ceremony, but for some odd reason I had always found the solemn liturgy and prayers of funerals to hold a strange attraction for me. Tom had teased me about that and told me to think about the fact that there was no payoff for us if people weren't having a good time. I smiled at the memory.

I looked up at the vaulted ceiling of the church, its bright blue expanse bordered by glittering, golden trim. The air was now thick with the smoke and fragrance of burning incense. I watched the priest and the altar boys as they approached the casket, in the center aisle near the communion railing. I wondered if the altar boys were friends, as Tom and I had been, and if their arms ached with the weight of the heavy, black-and-silver candle holders that needed to be held out in front of them, waist high. The priest circled the casket. He raised and lowered the censer as he prayed. The choir began to sing the familiar and brooding "Dies Irae." I had heard it so many times, I knew the lyrics by heart, and found myself singing them under my breath.

Dies irae! Dies illa!
Solvet saeclum in favilla
Teste David Cum Sibylla!

Quantus tremor est futures,
Quando judex est venturus
Cuncta stricte discussurus

Day of wrath! O day of mourning!
See fulfilled the prophets' warning,
Heaven and earth in ashes burning!

Oh what fear man's bosom rendeth,
When from heaven the Judge descendeth,
On whose sentence all dependeth.

The priest circled the casket for a second time as the altar boys stood at their posts near the communion rail. I watched and sang and prayed, but my thoughts kept drifting off to memories of Tom. The toughest kid I ever knew was gone. It all seemed so impossible. Dimly, I heard the priest again, this time praying in English. ". . . until the shadows lengthen, and the evening comes, and the busy world is hushed, and the fever of life is over, and our work is done and we rest in the sleep of peace."

When the service ended, I followed the procession of cars to St. Mary's Cemetery on Chicago Avenue. The temperature had moderated from earlier in the week, and hovered somewhere near the freezing mark. The sky was overcast, releasing a light but steady cascade of flakes. It fell dreamily, leaving only a delicate trace as it fell on the houses, streets, and fields. It floated lazily past the line of cars that moved solemnly along the main road of the cemetery, whirl-pooling from the back of each vehicle.

I parked at the rear of the halted procession. I watched the others emerge from their cars and walk slowly up a slight rise leading to the burial site. Some of them walked in pairs, their arms entwined, heads bowed as they comforted and steadied each other as they approached the grave.

I got out of my car. A steady wind began to blow as I looked out over the field of trees and headstones, barren and cold under the sunless sky. It was wrong, somehow, that Tom should be buried on such a day. It made no difference, of course, but I thought it should be sunny and green, with the smell of freshly mown grass and the air heavy with the promise of summer. I thought of a poem we had once read in English class. It was something by Edna St. Vincent Millay, about the loneliness of trees in winter.

I stood at the rear of the semi-circle of people gathered at the gravesite. The priest had already finished the prayers and closed the small black book in his hands.

He raised his eyes to the people. "This is a difficult time for all of us, especially the parents of God's servant, Tom. The mystery of death is always a great strain on those left behind, particularly when one is so young and their life is yet to be fulfilled. We feel angry at such times. We feel God has, in a sense, cheated us. But it is not our place to judge such things. It is not within our poor powers to understand such things. We must find strength in our faith, and in each other. We must pray that we will come to accept in our hearts what we cannot bring ourselves to understand."

An elderly couple stood just in front of me. The woman clung tightly to the man's arm, shaking her head back and forth. She leaned toward the little man. "It's such a pity," she whispered. "He was such a fine boy."

The man nodded and patted her arm.

"He was smart—and a hard worker, too."

The little man nodded again.

"The accident wasn't his fault at all. It was some crazy old man who hit him. I understand there was nothing left of his car. Just nothing left."

The little man again patted her arm and nodded.

I wondered who they were, these two who had come to mourn Tom's death. Then I heard the priest again.

"Tom's work is done now. His time among us is over. We must trust in the mystery of our faith and in the infinite wisdom of our God at these moments. We must comfort ourselves in knowing Tom is happy with the Lord."

I had never felt so alone in my life, and the priest's words didn't help. What he said sounded empty and hollow to me, without real meaning or understanding. Tom was gone, as if he had never existed. There was no faith that could change that. There was no comfort in mystery. There would only be memories to clutch tightly against the cold, unremitting wind and the onslaught of time.

When the service ended, I waited near the gravesite as most of the others headed back to their cars. I heard car doors slam shut in a series of chunking sounds, and the sound of protesting engines faded away on the icy wind as they left the cemetery. I waited for something I couldn't name. Maybe it was hope for some understanding of it all, some meaning that went beyond the random waste and sorrow. Finally, I turned away and headed for my car, leaving just a few mourners and Tom's family at the gravesite. As I approached the spot where I had parked, I sensed someone's presence. There was a shadowy movement to my left, just within my field of vision. I turned to face whoever intruded on my solitude.

Standing alone on the cold, snowy ground was Gloria. She raised one gloved hand and brushed her hair back behind her right ear. She put her hands in the slash pockets of her coat and looked directly into my eyes. I stood transfixed, holding my breath, afraid the slightest movement might somehow destroy the moment and cause her to run away. "I'm so sorry, Will," she said. Her eyes glistened as she waited a moment to speak again.

"Gloria . . ."

"About Tom—about everything. I'm so sorry. I looked for you at the church, but I didn't see you. I wanted to tell you—"

Before she could finish what she was about to say, I grabbed her and held her tight. "Oh, God, Gloria."

She hugged me in return, and then leaned back in my arms, so she could look at me as she spoke. "This must be horrible for you. I mean, I don't think I've ever known friends who were as close as you and Tom."

I pulled her to me again. I held her so tight, I didn't know if it was her heart I felt beating or my own. I kept holding onto her until I felt the muscles knot in my arms. "God, Gloria, I've wanted so much to explain everything to you—and then this. It's just too much to . . ."

She leaned back again and raised her face to mine. She brushed a few wind-swept hairs away from her eyes. "No, Will, you don't need to explain anything. I was being an idiot. I know that now."

"But, I still want you to know about—"

"No, Will, I know about everything. I'm the one who needs to explain."

"I don't understand."

"Just yesterday, Jean O'Hara found me and told me everything about that night—and how you wouldn't go swimming and didn't want to be there. She told it all to me."

"Jean O'Hara did that?"

"Yes."

Twenty-Seven

THE FOLLOWING WEEK DEE ARRIVED home for the Thanksgiving holiday. It was good to see her again and talk with her about all that had happened. I told her about Tom and about reconciling with Gloria. She listened patiently, as always, but she was so excited about her boyfriend, Don, coming to visit on Friday, her ebullient mood could hardly be suppressed, even for a moment. She seemed to float about the house, gliding behind Mom or Dad and chattering endlessly about school and Don and the upcoming holidays, so energized and happy that not even the weight of a lost life could bring her to the ground.

Gloria and I had two coinciding days free of work that week, and I spent as much time with her as possible. Her mother seemed happy to see me back in their house and kept offering me things to eat: cookies, pitted cherries, homemade ice cream, whatever was available. I thought of these treats as her wordless apology for having misjudged me. Mr. Scully, on the other hand, was his usual taciturn self and seemed less than thrilled with my reappearance. Gloria came to our house as well. She and Dee appeared to establish an immediate bond, now and then making quiet asides to one another and laughing at something that wasn't to be shared with the rest of us.

And when Don came to visit on Friday of that week, he and my father talked excitedly about a young senator from Massachusetts, John F. Kennedy, who they believed had a real chance of becoming the first Catholic president. Despite their allegiance to Senator Humphrey of our own state, and mindful of his presidential ambitions, their excitement about the potential for a Catholic, Democratic president clearly overshadowed those old political loyalties. So, it was a week of reconciliation and closeness and shared hopes, and should have been a time of unfettered happiness, but it wasn't—at least, not for me.

There wasn't a single day, and most days not a single hour, that I didn't think about Tom. In my thoughts I kept turning over what had happened, as if I were examining the pieces of some bizarre, unsolvable puzzle. I talked mostly with Gloria about it, though the truth was I couldn't really articulate my feelings. They went beyond my own expectations, reaching strange corners of thought I hadn't anticipated and over which I seemed to exert no control. I thought about the moment when the cars collided and the reality of Tom's body being crushed and torn apart. How much had he been aware of what was happening? How long was he in pain? What last thoughts had he held before his final breath? It was all so wrong, so impossible. Death came to grandparents or elderly aunts and uncles and frail, gray, unknown inhabitants of nursing homes and hospitals. Your friends weren't snatched from life. Children didn't die before their parents. But it was true. That he was gone was beyond belief, yet every day confirmed that fact and every place I went was a vivid reminder of his absence.

I thought, too, about what he and I had been taught about death from the time we were little children together at Holy Rosary, how the soul went on to eternal suffering or eternal joy depending on the life we had led and the acts we had committed or omitted, as if it was all sensible and under our control, and we were all given equal strengths and equally difficult challenges. Only our choices, our willful decisions, made any difference in our fate. I remembered the blue *Baltimore Catechism* Tom and I had studied at Holy Rosary School, and the illustration of three milk bottles representing the soul and its state of grace. A pure white bottle of milk represented pure grace, a readiness for heaven. A bottle marked with areas of gray demonstrated the soul blemished with venial sin, with entry to heaven merely delayed until purification was performed. A completely black bottle reflected mortal sin and eternal damnation, unless first forgiven through the sacrament of confession. Tom had looked across the aisle at me and said in a whisper that he liked chocolate milk best. Tom, the rebel, the wise guy, the brawler, had been a better person than anyone knew. Tom, my friend and protector, who had known only a hardscrabble life and expected nothing better than an indifferent world, had been determined to be just as tough as life required. And he hadn't even been allowed to live out his years, whimsically and brutally destroyed by a chance encounter. What did that mean? What possible purpose had been served? How had God been glorified by Tom's truncated life, his few years of awareness and struggle?

I knew my brooding introspection made me unfit for most company, so I did what I could to avoid others, with the exception of Gloria. While I hadn't been able to fully explain to her what a cataclysmic shift I felt in the order and logic of existence, she seemed to sense much of what was troubling me without words of explanation. She was silent at times when I most needed silence and reassuring when I most needed just a word or gesture of understanding. But even her patience with my inner turmoil, I found, had its limits.

Less than a week before Christmas, Gloria and I sat at a corner table in Beek's Pizza as the juke box thumped out a heavy beat, punctuated by shouts and laughter from the crowded tables. It had been a good day, or at least better than most over the last month. Gloria and I had gone Christmas shopping earlier and for most of the day I hadn't been haunted by the memory of Tom. We had just ordered our pizza when I felt a cold draft as the door swung open. I glanced toward the front of the shack and saw Pipsqueak Preston burst through the doorway with several girls in tow. I quickly looked away from him and shifted my position so that I was mostly hidden by Gloria. My maneuver was more obvious than I thought. "What is it?" Gloria said.

"Nothing, a guy just came in that I don't want to talk to."

"Who?" she said, as she turned to glance around the room.

"A guy named Pipsqueak Preston. He's someone Tom knew. If he sees me he's going to want to talk about Tom, and I don't want to talk with him about any of what happened."

Gloria searched my face, her dark eyes penetrating and sympathetic. "Do you want to leave?"

"No. No, it's okay. I don't think he saw me, anyway. Let's have our pizza. If he comes over, he comes over. It's just . . . I just would rather not talk to him."

"Okay, Will, if you're sure you want to stay."

"Yeah, it's fine. Everything's fine."

I picked up my glass of Coke and took a deep drink. I leaned to my right to peek around Gloria's shoulder to see where Pipsqueak was sitting. I was relieved to see that he and his friends had found a table near the door, his back to me. I relaxed a bit and took another drink without looking at Gloria.

"I don't know what to do, Will," Gloria said, her voice low and full of melancholy.

"What? What are you talking about?"

Gloria leaned forward, reached across the table and grasped my free hand. She squeezed it tightly. "Will, I know this has been a terrible time for you . . . and I just don't know what to do. I don't know how to help." She shook my hand as she spoke, as if she needed to communicate each word with physical force.

"I'm fine," I said. I wanted to pull my hand free and tell her to leave me alone. The truth was, no one understood. No one could possibly understand, not even Gloria.

She let go of my hand, as if my thoughts had been spoken aloud. "Will," she said, "I've never lost anyone so close to me—not anyone I really knew. My father died before I was ever able to even see him, so I know it isn't the same thing at all, but . . ." Gloria fell silent as the waitress arrived with our pizza.

"Anything else here?" the waitress said without looking in our direction.

"No," I said.

She slapped the bill on the table. "Pay at the register," she said as she turned away.

I pulled two wedges from the pie and put one on Gloria's plate and one on my own. I wanted to bite into the pizza immediately, so that eating might momentarily put the conversation on hold, but I needed to let the slice cool. I recalled the time I had burned my mouth and how Tom had teased me about it.

"I know it isn't the same, Will," Gloria said as she continued with her thought, "but I think I have some idea how you feel.

"When I was a little girl I was so angry that I had no father and all the stories my mom told me about him, in some ways, just made everything worse. I would look at old black-and-white pictures of him and try to imagine what it would have been like to have him with us at home, what it would have been like to see him walk through the door and rush into his arms and be his little girl. What did he smell like? Would his beard have been all scratchy on my cheek? And the more I thought about it, the sadder and angrier I got. And I knew no one understood how I felt or what I was going through—not even my mom. I didn't care if he was a war hero. I didn't care if he had saved other people. I didn't care if he had saved the whole world. He was my dad, and I had never gotten to see him or touch his hand or hear his voice. That was wrong—and nothing could make it right, not ever."

As I listened, my thoughts raced back and forth from what she was telling me to memories of Tom, and I felt my throat grow tight and hot. "What . . . what are you trying to tell me?" I said, my voice husky with emotion.

"It's just that it took me a long time to realize a few things I should have understood from the start."

I picked up my slice of pizza and blew on it. For some reason, what she was telling me had nearly brought me to tears and I didn't fully understand why. I stared at my pizza slice, afraid to look at her. I managed to get out just two words before I bit into the pizza. "Like what?" I said.

Gloria was silent for so long that I finally looked up at her. She was watching me intently and had evidently waited for me to make eye contact with her, as if she would only tell me what she had learned if she knew my attention was unwavering. "Everyone dies, Will. They die whether they are young or strong or loved or hated or lonely or rich or poor. They die every day in every possible way—by accident or illness or war. And there is nothing that can change it and nothing we can do about it."

"I know that," I said, my words broken and angry.

"I know you do, Will. So did I, even as a little girl—in my mind, but not in my gut. Now you know it in a way that you never did before, and I have some idea how much it hurts."

I couldn't look at her face any longer, those dark, penetrating, uncompromising eyes. I looked beyond her at the other tables, at the glowing, brightly colored jukebox, at Pipsqueak and the girls gathered at his table. Everyone was so young, so full of passion. The room pulsated with their raw energy. The front door opened again and a wintery breeze swept through the room and cooled my burning eyes. Finally, I looked back at Gloria.

"I suppose, in a way, I was lucky," she said. "I never got to know my dad, so I only missed someone I had just heard about and could only imagine. It wasn't like you, losing someone you'd been friends with practically your whole life."

"Maybe we should just eat," I said. The words came out more angrily than I intended.

"Don't be mad, Will. I just want to tell you what it took me so long to figure out, and that is that much of what we feel—or at least what I felt—I finally realized was not sorrow for my father, but for myself."

For the first time since I had known her, I was truly angry with Gloria. "What? What are you saying—that I'm just feeling sorry for myself, that I didn't care about Tom? That's pretty damned mean and unfair, Gloria."

She reached across the table to touch my hand. She no longer looked strong and unyielding, but vulnerable and sad. "No, Will, that isn't what I'm trying to say at all. I think you do have reasons to feel sorry for yourself. Why shouldn't you? I know it's been a terrible loss for you."

I pulled my hand away. "Damn it, Gloria. Let's just eat."

Her arm remained across the table, her hand still reaching out for mine. "I probably said it all wrong. I'm just trying to say that you have to find a way to keep living your life. You can't stop enjoying everything because of what happened to Tom. It was horrible and stupid and made no sense at all, but your sorrow won't change any of it—and it only hurts the people who care about you."

I choked down some food and looked at her, her hand still reaching out across the table. "I can't just turn my feelings off like a light. It isn't so easy, you know."

"I know it isn't. I know it isn't easy at all, and I know that it takes time. I'm just . . . I'm trying to say that Tom's troubles are behind him now, and you need to be thinking about your own life and not let yourself be destroyed by what happened—not let it weigh you down and crush you. I don't mean to be mean, I really don't." She paused and swallowed hard before she continued with renewed effort. "Hurting you again is the last thing in the world I would ever want to do, but I hate seeing you like this. I hate seeing you just . . . I don't know, turning away from everything." Her voice was tremulous now. "It's like you've become lost somewhere inside yourself and I can't find a way to reach you."

She didn't say any more. We ate the rest of our meal in silence, in that shadowy corner of the pizza shack, each caught up in our own reflections. Perhaps, I thought, she was right. I could never make sense of what happened to Tom, not if I agonized over it for a year or ten years or a lifetime. And I knew too that I must find a way out of my sullen ruminations. It did no good. There was no profit in it for Tom or for me or for anyone I knew or cared about. And yet it would be a struggle, a long war of attrition between reason and emotion. At last, I could feel my anger subsiding as I turned her words and their intent over in my thoughts.

When we left the pizza shack, the evening was cold and windless, with a light, fine snow that fell straight to the ground. We stepped out the door, still caught up in our silence, neither of us seeming to know how to end it. We walked beneath the lighted, crown-shaped sign that spelled out "Beek—King of Pizza," and headed to the parking lot and my car. The newly fallen snow squeaked and crunched beneath our feet. As we neared the car, I put my arm around Gloria's shoulders and drew her close to me, no longer consumed by anger and sorrow but by my affection for her. She turned toward me and held up her face, aglow in the remnants of light from a distant street lamp and the unbroken stream of traffic moving along Hiawatha Avenue. Her lips bore just the slightest hint of a smile as she blinked away the snow. "I'm sorry, Will, I was only trying to help."

"I know," I said and held her tight. "I know you were."

* * * * *

OVER THE DAYS AND WEEKS THAT FOLLOWED, I did my best not to forget Tom and all we had been to each other, but rather to gain a larger, less mournful perspective, one that is so hard to achieve at seventeen years—and, really, perhaps at any age. The routine of work and school and dating was both an aid and a barrier to reaching some emotional balance. The rush of each day kept me constantly occupied, but nearly everything I did and everywhere I went carried a memory of him, and when I visited somewhere he had never been, I was struck by that fact, too. As the weeks stretched out beyond the holidays, there was a day—one otherwise unremarkable afternoon at work, as I laughed at something Bill Freeman said—when I realized the sting of the past autumn had been blunted. I couldn't mark the day or the hour it had happened, only the moment of its realization. And even that moment brought a special sadness of its own. Life was not as it once had been. I realized that. I also came to realize that while the memory of Tom would not go on haunting me every hour or every day, the world was now a more sober place and had lost a certain luster it would likely never regain. And one bright morning, I also learned that while the wound of his death was no longer fresh and raw, it could easily be torn open again.

I was hurrying to my second hour class when I saw Jean O'Hara coming toward me, her bright, shiny red ponytail bouncing in rhythm to her hurried steps. She appeared focused on some distant point in the hallway and I waved my hand in front of her face to catch her attention. "Hey, Jean," I said as she neared. "Jean," I called out a second time.

She stopped and looked up at me, eyebrows arched high in surprise. "Will. Hey, how are you?"

"I'm fine," I said. "Hey, I've been meaning to thank you for what you did."

She looked bewildered as students rushed around us, one bumping her so hard that she nearly dropped her books. "Thank me?"

"Yeah. I mean, I know it was months ago, but I wanted to thank you for explaining to Gloria what happened last summer. You know, about that night we were out at Lake Nokomis."

"Oh, yeah, that."

"It meant a lot to me, Jean. It really brought Gloria and me back together."

"Yeah, I know." She juggled one of her books as it nearly slipped to the floor, flashing a quick smile as she regained control of the stack. "Yeah, well, you're welcome." She smiled again, apparently uncertain about what to do or say next. "Well, see you around, I guess."

"Yeah, see you around." I smiled back at her. "Thanks again."

I was just about to turn and continue on down the hall when Jean spoke again. "That was really funny, you know?"

"What was funny?"

"Tom asking me to explain that to her just a few hours before he . . . before his accident. I mean it was that same afternoon. That seemed sort of really weird and creepy to me. I was going to do it anyway, 'cause I promised him I would, but when I heard about what happened to him, I made sure I did it right away the next time I had a chance to see her. I don't know, it was just a really weird feeling."

I felt as if I had been struck in the chest. I became light-headed and unable for a moment or two to catch my breath. "Tom? Tom asked you to explain to Gloria?"

"Yeah. I guess I thought you knew that. He said I had to tell her because she wouldn't talk to you at all, and she'd never believe him." She paused for a moment, clutching her books more tightly. "You okay? You look like you don't feel so good."

"No. I mean, yeah, I'm fine." I took a deep breath. "I didn't know that . . . about Tom asking you to do that."

"No?" Her brow furrowed and her bewildered look deepened. "Huh, I thought you did. Hey, well anyways, I'm glad it all turned out okay for you. But, God, that was really awful about Tom, wasn't it?"

My thoughts were in riot and I found that I could barely follow or respond to what she was saying. "Yeah, it was awful."

"Yeah, he was a great guy." She shifted her problematic stack of books again, evidently making a final, critical adjustment for her continued journey down the corridor. "Listen, I really got to go, but it was great to talk to you again. See you around." She took a few steps and turned back. "Oh, hey, good luck with Gloria," she said over her shoulder.

"Thanks," I said. I stood there as the river of students flowed around me and ran off into the doorways and corridors and stairwells, until the warning bell and, at last, the final bell rang.

Twenty-Eight

When the holidays were over and Dee had returned to school, the Minnesota winter accelerated toward spring, twilight arriving later and later until finally the first buds on the trees and a sustained warmth in the wind marked the end of the bitterly cold weather. The sun's arc lengthened and grew higher each week, burning off snow and wispy morning clouds and once again greening the lawns and fields and parkways. The trees lining the city streets leafed out in shades of emerald and forest green and reached out to one another across the dark, gritty avenues of city pavement. The air grew heavy with the smell of lilac and freshly mown grass and all the fragrant promises of summer.

Junior year ended with the signing of yearbooks and loosely laid plans to see classmates at the little beach at Lake Nokomis, Porky's drive-in, Beek's pizza, Keller's, or any of a dozen other hangouts. The *Tiger* annuals were rife with brief, written remembrances of the academic year just ended: who had been a clown in class, which couples had broken up, which games were won, which parties attended, which friends made, which secrets shared. Countless jokes were written in yearbooks about their owners managing against incredible odds and personal shortcomings to complete the year, cautions against consuming too much beer or smoking too much, warnings about spending too much time working or too much time at the beach. There were musings and coy remarks about new boyfriends or girlfriends and congratulations on becoming a senior and advancing to a final year at South High. Teachers signed the books too, recalling successes of the past year and wishing each student a safe, relaxing summer.

For Gloria and for me, summer meant working full-time, seizing every opportunity we had to be together and saving for whatever future we might envision beyond high school. We were, suddenly, going to enter our senior year. It was, at once, hopeful and exhilarating and frightening and sobering. The world beyond school was only one year away—and drew closer each day. At work, Jim began to press me more and more about my plans after completion of high school, with a renewed enthusiasm for his belief that I would be wise to consider a vocational school where I could learn hotel and restaurant cooking and prepare myself for life as a chef. I knew I didn't want that, but I was still uncertain about what I did want and what I should do after graduation. My future was an occasional topic at home as well, with both my mother and father leaning strongly toward my applying for entrance to the University of Minnesota, though neither of them had any specific ideas about a particular area of study or a career path, but simply thought it was "the right thing to do." My greatest concern was that whatever I might choose to do, it shouldn't interfere—or at worst should only minimally interfere—with my relationship with Gloria. So I remained somewhat directionless in terms of a solid plan for the coming year, with only the vaguest sense as to what actions I might take in regard to my own future. And, really, a year still seemed like adequate time to make whatever decisions would need to be made.

For the most part, time away from work was sun-drenched and untroubled and not filled with angst about the future. Gloria and I spent as many hours as possible at the little beach at Nokomis with a crowd of people from school. There was the July Fourth celebration at Powderhorn Park, and even a night when we doubled with Bill Freeman from work and a girl from Central High who had been newly hired as a waitress at Keller's. For my parents, summer held challenges and meaning very separate from my world.

Dee had decided to spend most of the summer in St. Cloud, where she had been offered a job by the college. Her working there not only provided an income for the next school year but had the additional benefit of decreasing her tuition. She came home on weekends, when she could, usually hitching a ride for the sixty-five-mile trip with one group or another of fellow students. On weekends when she didn't come home to visit, she spent what time she could either going to Duluth to see Don, or staying near campus while he traveled to St. Cloud to visit her. Her nomadic existence and sporadic appearances at home made her visits all the more a cause for celebration but also, I'm sure, were bittersweet occasions for Mom and Dad. Their daughter was now even more detached and independent than when she first left for college, and they must have felt both pride in her becoming an adult and a subtle pang of loss.

My father was consumed by politics that summer, closely following the fortunes of Senator Kennedy from Massachusetts. When our own Senator Humphrey gave up seeking the nomination after he lost the West Virginia primary, Humphrey's momentary and uncharacteristic cynicism and bitterness were captured in his reference to the Kennedy family's wealth and influence, noting that, "You can't beat Jack's jack." My father's passion and interest were rewarded in mid-July, when the Democratic National Convention in Los Angeles celebrated the nomination of only the second Catholic in the nation's history to run for president. My father informed me that it was probably a good thing that the only other Catholic nominee, Al Smith, had lost the race in 1928. Had he won, he assured me, Catholics would have been blamed for the Great Depression. He listened closely as Senator Kennedy accepted the nomination and spoke of the new frontier of the 1960s and called upon Americans to sacrifice for their country. I wondered later, when I reflected on it a bit, if my father didn't feel some slight sense of irony and embarrassment when, in his acceptance speech, Senator Kennedy said, "I hope that no American, considering the really critical issues facing this country, will waste his franchise by voting either for me or against me solely on account of my religious affiliation. It is not relevant."

The week before Labor Day and the start of our senior year, Gloria and I spent an entire day at the State Fair, enjoying one last outing of summer vacation. We gorged ourselves on fair cuisine: corn dogs, Tom Thumb donuts, caramel apples, taffy and nearly anything that could be deep-fried and impaled on a stick. We walked for hours, touring the animal barns, the Grandstand displays, the agriculture building, the education building, the fine arts building and even stopped for a few moments at one of the political booths urging voters to elect Kennedy and join him on the New Frontier. Toward dusk, we headed to the midway and the Royal American Shows.

We walked along the carnival midway, the lights of the rides and game tents already lit. When we reached the sideshow tent, the sword swallower had just finished demonstrating his skill and was taking a deep bow before an appreciative crowd. He quickly left the stage and disappeared behind a purple curtain that led inside the enormous tent. The sideshow barker immediately began urging the crowd inside to see wonders never seen before—at a one-time discount price. "Don't walk up and down the midway and think you can come back later and get in at these prices. For this show only, everyone gets in at children's prices. C'mon, c'mon," he shouted in a pressured, graveled voice. "See the bearded lady, the woman with alligator skin and the world's tiniest man. Everyone gets in at children's prices—this show only."

We continued our walk along the midway as the sun began to fade below the treetops and dusty tents. We watched several people fail at games of skill and spotted a shill being repeatedly awarded several packs of cigarettes, though he had failed to even once successfully pitch a wooden ring onto the neck of a Coke bottle. "Should I point that out to anyone?" I said to Gloria.

She struck me playfully on the arm. "Don't start any trouble," she whispered and laughed.

The only ride we had taken all day was one not on the carnival midway, but located on a street corner in the main body of the fairgrounds and had been there since 1913. Ye Old Mill, a tunnel of love with wooden boats that meandered through a darkened chamber at the leisurely pace of the mill-driven water, had been one of our first stops. Once we were in the tunnel, it seemed such an obvious and unsophisticated romantic gesture, I had kissed Gloria in only a joking and apologetic way. Now, with the day and the summer nearing its end, I took her by the hand and headed toward the ferris wheel. "Before we leave, let's see the fair from up there," I said.

As we rose to the full height of the ride, the blue-green horizon of trees beyond the midway had darkened to a shadowy gray expanse dappled with the yellow lights of buildings and street lamps and food stands. Below us, the noise of the crowd and the roustabouts and carnies became an indistinct and distant humming that blended with the whirring of the motors and generators of the Royal American Shows trailers. As we descended with each turning of the wheel, our senses were flooded with the colors and smells and sounds of the carnival, before we rose once again into the clear night air and a cool breeze that swept high above the earth. We were near the top of the rotation when the wheel slowed to a stop as riders began to depart the seats beneath us. With my left arm, I pulled Gloria close to me. I took her face in my hands and kissed her forehead and mouth and neck. I put my arms around her and hugged her. I could feel our car sway dangerously as I pressed my cheek against hers and whispered in her ear that I loved her.

"I love you too, Will, I do," she replied.

I held on and felt the smooth warmth of her cheek against mine as I looked out at the night sky and first faint glimmer of stars in the east. I had never felt so exquisitely happy in my life—a feeling so intense I could barely contain or endure it. And I had never been more acutely aware than at that moment how fragile and impermanent such bliss could be.

*****

SENIOR YEAR BEGAN WITH THE SMELL of freshly waxed floors and the sound of bustling students and shouted greetings and slamming locker doors. There was catching up to do with people I hadn't seen since the previous year—or had seen only occasionally at the beach or at a party—textbooks to wrap in orange and black South High Tiger dust covers and classes to locate. And this year Gloria and I would attend homecoming, just as we had promised each other. So, September swept by at dizzying speed, with the month ending in a homecoming defeat at the hands of the Roosevelt Teddies, though the loss of the game did little to dampen our enthusiasm for the dance. Gloria looked stunning in a green taffeta dress and I wore my first suit—navy blue and made of worsted wool.

There was excitement that fall, at least for some, with news that a professional football team would begin to play in Minnesota with the 1961 NFL season. Given my somewhat checkered and discouraging history with the game, I was not one of those who found the news to be of particular interest or cause for any great moment of elation. Of greater general interest were plans for a school-wide mock presidential election.

The entire student body would vote for the Kennedy or Nixon ticket, and there was talk of top political leaders possibly attending an all-school election rally. The rumors were right. Senator Hubert H. Humphrey, representing the Democratic Party, and Minneapolis Mayor P.K. Peterson, representing the Republican Party, attended an October rally in the school auditorium. Student representatives debated foreign policy and homerooms, representing various states, carried banners and signs in support of one candidate or the other, or both. "Wisconsin Needs Nixon-Lodge." "Kennedy for President." Four-cornered banners were held aloft that read "California" or "Illinois" or "Florida." The impassioned and voluble speeches by the senator and mayor were cheered wildly by the students and the auditorium reverberated to a raucous energy beyond any I had ever seen at a pep rally. It was clear, I thought, that the school's political guests were both amused and heartened by what they saw and heard.

On Friday, November 4, the entire student body voted. In what later appeared to be a prescient selection, Kennedy was the victor in our mock election. The national vote, however, was much closer and much slower in revealing the winner. When the vote was finally tallied, Kennedy had won by only one-tenth of one percent of the popular vote. With a margin of only a little over one-hundred-thousand votes, John F. Kennedy became the first Catholic president of the United States. My father was ecstatic, and even high school students who had never paid much attention to politics were suddenly captivated by the young, witty new president as he embarked on his New Frontier. Somehow, politics had become interesting—or at least, the people in politics were interesting. Commercial shops were not immune to his charm, either. Liemandt's clothing store in downtown Minneapolis had a full-scale color cardboard image of the President in a Hart, Schaffner and Marx suit. As you entered the men's suit department on the second floor, just to the right stood President Kennedy in a blue pinstriped suit, beaming at all who exited the elevator.

I continued to work at the Shadow Box throughout senior year, listening to Jim's wide-ranging opinions on everything from Gopher football to the new Kennedy Administration. He seemed to have given up on trying to persuade me to study hotel and restaurant cooking and brought up the topic of my future less and less until it was no longer a subject of discussion at all. By the time the holidays had come and gone, I had decided that my best option was to test for college and hopefully enter the University of Minnesota's school of Science and Liberal Arts. While I wasn't certain what major I might want to study, I could remain close to Gloria and there was time to sample courses and discover where my interests might take me. Gloria was also planning to attend the University of Minnesota and was certain she wanted to major in English. I knew I was really doing little more than biding my time, but life seemed unhurried that year. We had time to grow and experiment and explore—all the time in the world.

Then, on a warm, clear June evening, three-hundred-fifty-six of us, with family and friends in attendance, gathered in the South High auditorium for the last time. There were speeches and the Pledge of Allegiance and the choir sang "You'll Never Walk Alone." And finally, just before the awarding of diplomas, we all rose to sing the alma mater. At first the voices were tentative and thin, but they grew stronger and filled the auditorium during the last stanza, as if we all had conspired to punctuate this final moment together.

Though years will come when we are gone from Old South High
They ne'er will take a loyal heart from Old South High
Though silent time steals fast upon us, love is young,
In spite of years, of foes and fears, thy praises shall be sung.

The ceremony ended as we exited the auditorium to the strains of "Pomp and Circumstance," our blue robes waving about our knees and ankles, diplomas in hand, our smiles unrestrained in the flash of cameras held by rhapsodic parents. We were off on those first real steps into adulthood. Some of us would soon leave for the military, others were off to college or trade schools, still others would enter the workforce for the very first time. We had made it. We were through—done with high school and foolish constraints and the things of childhood.

The 1960s stretched out before us, ours to embrace and shape and define. There was a young, vibrant new president in office, and the nation was at peace. We stood on the threshold of a new decade—our decade—full of untold promise, with no portentous signs of what was to come—at least none we could discern. We were free to follow our dreams and ambitions, no matter how majestic or mundane. On that night, in that place, we were young and unafraid and believed that life was, perhaps, perfectible, and that we might make of ourselves anything we could imagine. From that starting point, with the blue-black evening sky awash with brilliant, crystalline stars, we fanned out into a new, undiscovered world—accomplished students, tough guys, budding politicians, bad girls, athletes, dreamers. All of us but one.

Epilogue

READING OF JUNIOR KANDOWSKI'S DEATH brought back all those memories, most vividly of those bitter and disconsolate weeks following Tom's accident. The richness and detail of those long ago days surprised me, as if some special, secret place in my mind had been unlocked and all the contents had rushed forth, free of the usual distortion and atrophy of time. It was all so clear, so immediate and familiar—but seen now from the vantage point and biases of a man more than half a century older. In retrospect, the O'Hara twins, the poor, sweet, bad girls of South High, now seemed so naïve and innocent. Old Jim, who had been such an enigma to me, who had lost his religion but never his capacity for faith, who had unintentionally taught me that it is not necessarily what we believe that finally binds us together but what we doubt, had now been dead for more than thirty years and resting on that gentle, grassy rise. Mrs. Bridges, Coach Phillips, Bill Freeman, Mr. Horton, Pipsqueak Preston, all the personalities who had been so vital, paraded before me once again.

More fleetingly, I thought of the years after high school, especially those early, turbulent and horrific times following graduation. On a Friday in November of 1963, I had been on my way from the university to my job at the restaurant when I heard that President Kennedy had been shot. By the time I reached Lake Street there was already an evening "extra" paper headlining the assassination in Dallas. I remembered working that weekend and the restaurant being filled to capacity nearly every hour it was open—but the crowds so in shock that no one was speaking. People needed to be near one another but were too stunned and grieved to utter a word. And then the war, the endless war in Vietnam. Some classmates died in the war and others went to prison for protesting it. Some returned to a life of permanent impairment while others didn't return at all. Some remained scarred for life because they had evaded the draft or had violently opposed the war. I had been lucky, I suppose. I had joined the Navy Reserve while still in college and was stationed at a base in Japan after graduation. All that time, Gloria had waited. She had written to me every week for two years, without fail.

The decade wore on, growing more violent and divisive each year. The roiling division of racial hatred and political discord led to more assassinations—Martin Luther King, Jr., Robert F. Kennedy—and riots and civil unrest as we had never seen it. There were a few personal bright spots in those years—Dee and Don marrying and Dad and Mom retiring to a life of hard-earned leisure—moments that pushed the larger horrors off stage for a brief time. It seemed that it all had culminated in the bloody Democratic Convention in Chicago in August of 1968, as if that was the point at which all sides finally backed away, realizing the country could no longer survive such internecine violence. For me, it seemed our troubled decade had come to a premature and welcome end in 1968.

In the early evening of the day I read of Junior Kandowski's death, I found Gloria returned from our daughter's house and preparing dinner for the two of us in the kitchen. She was silhouetted as the setting sun shone through the patio doors and glanced off countertops and appliances. I watched her for a moment, unseen, and pictured her as she had been when we first met: the shoulder-length, auburn hair, the dark, penetrating eyes, and the pinkish, youthful cheeks. Her hair was short now and gray, with no attempt to color or conceal the process of aging. Her cheeks were less full, and lines of many years of work and the stress of life had been etched around her eyes, but the eyes themselves had not changed. They were still bright with intelligence and understanding and a certain look of sympathy that could instantly let me know that while the whole world might conspire against me, she was unquestionably on my side. I moved into the light. "How was everything at Christy's?"

"Oh, Will, I didn't know you were there," she said, and momentarily halted her work at the cutting board.

"Sorry, I didn't mean to startle you."

"Everyone was just fine," she said and returned to the task of slicing red and yellow peppers. "I can't believe how much that child talks," she said, referring to our grandson of just two years. "And he wants to know everything. 'Gammy, what's this? Gammy, what's that?' I really think he is an exceptionally bright little boy."

I couldn't help but smile as I thought of him, and thought of how all grandparents must feel very much the same way. "Yeah, Mike's my guy." I reached out to snatch a piece of pepper.

"Will, please, wait for dinner."

I withdrew my hand, but not before I had managed to grab a slice of red pepper. "Do you remember a kid we went to high school with named James Kandowski? Back then everybody called him Junior."

Gloria stopped her work for a second time. She furrowed her brow slightly and looked at some point just over my shoulder. "James Kandowski," she repeated in a low, confidential tone as she continued to stare beyond me. "The name sounds familiar, but I'm not sure. Why do you ask?"

"His obituary was in the paper today."

Oh, no," she said. "He was in our class?"

"Yeah, I played football with him in sophomore year—big guy, always smiling. We weren't great buddies or anything, but he was one of the most decent kids I ever knew. I got to thinking about him and about some really fine things he did when we were young. Looking back, I don't know why we didn't become better friends. He was a great kid."

Gloria remained still, her knife and right hand resting on the cutting board, her left hand on her hip. "Yes, I think I do remember him. Junior—Junior Kandowski, I think I had him in my sophomore history class. Big, bright kid, kind of broad-faced, very polite?"

"Yeah, that sounds like him. Anyway, I thought maybe we could at least go to his visitation. I know it sounds kind of crazy, I wasn't ever in touch with him after high school and we've never even been to a class reunion, but I just . . . I'd like to pay my respects. I don't know, it's just something I'd like to do." The idea of attending services for Junior now sounded more eccentric than it had seemed before I expressed it aloud.

"When is the visitation?" she asked as she resumed her work.

Gloria's question was matter-of-fact, as if my desire to attend the service was the most natural thing in the world. It heartened me just to hear the way she asked the question. "It's this Friday evening from six until nine."

"But we're taking care of Mike that night, remember?"

"Oh, that's right," I said. I had completely forgotten our promise to our daughter and son-in-law to baby-sit so they could enjoy a night out. "Well, it was just kind of a crazy idea. Just some wild, sentimental thinking, I guess."

"No, you know what? You should go. You can meet me out at Christy's afterward. Mike and I will be just fine until you get there."

"Oh, it isn't that important, really."

Gloria looked up from her work. "I think you should go, Will. I think it's sweet of you to want to go, and you'll be glad later that you went. It's just a couple of hours out of your life, and you'll regret it if you don't go."

I knew from her voice and the steady, uncompromising look in her eyes that she was convinced it was the right thing for me to do. She waited for my response as I took a bite of my illicit slice of pepper. "Okay. You're right," I finally said. "I think I will go."

* * * * *

EARLY FRIDAY EVENING, AFTER GLORIA had left for our daughter's house, I drove east into Minneapolis and the funeral chapel on Lyndale Avenue. The summer evening was warm, with the sun drifting slowly across a cloudless sky. When I left the freeway and began the drive north along Lyndale, I turned off the car's air conditioning, opened my window and let the summer breeze wash over me. After a mile or so, I stopped for a red light. A group of teenagers was crossing the street from the west side to the east—three girls and two boys. All of them wore shorts, tank tops and sandals, and they hollered and laughed and poked at each other as they crossed. One of the girls broke away from the group, then turned quickly, faced them as she walked backward and laughed uproariously at some private joke. I smiled as I watched this enthusiastic little group, until I heard the smaller of the two boys speak. "What's that old man staring at?" he said. He looked only at his friends, but spoke the words loudly enough for me to hear them. I was so engrossed in thoughts of Junior and the vision of exuberant teenagers on a summer evening that it took a second or two before I realized I was the old man of his concern. I looked away and focused on the traffic light.

Within ten minutes I was at the funeral chapel. There were two parlors inside the one-story, cream-colored brick building. A small, black sign with white lettering indicated that the visitation for James Kandowski was in the room on the left. I entered the room and immediately felt the body heat of those crowded inside. I signed a visitors' book sitting atop a pedestal to my right before walking slowly through the crowded room, thinking I might see someone I knew. Everyone seemed busy visiting in hushed tones, some smiling, a few crying freely.

Near the center of the room was a meandering line of people waiting to speak with a woman I assumed to be Junior's widow. She was tall, trim and looked fit. At a distance, her age was only betrayed by gray hair that was streaked here and there by fading strands of brown. My first reaction, though only momentary, was to wonder why Junior had been married to such an older woman. As at the stop light on my way to the visitation, my confusion was quickly set right. A younger man stood next to her, his bearing and physical appearance reminiscent of Junior. A girl of perhaps eight or nine years in a long, dark blue dress, with chestnut-colored hair that fell to the middle of her back, kept throwing her arms around the young man and making exhortations I could not hear. The girl would walk away, then return a minute or so later, throw her arms around the man's waist and renew her plea.

I busied myself by walking slowly about the room, viewing photographs and inscriptions on cards attached to floral arrangements. A television in one corner of the room looped a video about Junior's life, most of it a voiceover with illustrative photographs. I watched the video briefly and couldn't help but smile at the pictures of Junior in his high school football uniform and a graduation photo from South High. I continued my journey about the room, periodically searching the crowd unsuccessfully for a familiar face.

I eventually found myself at the far end of the parlor, where Junior lay in an open casket, flanked at both his head and feet by great arcs of bright flowers. I had, from as far back as I could remember, secretly found the open display of the deceased to be somehow barbaric and of questionable taste, but despite these personal misgivings I lingered there. I looked down on Junior. I tried to see beyond the thin hair and the pale skin to some semblance of the boy I had once known. Gradually it came to me. I could see again the vibrant young man from so long ago. "Junior," I whispered, "I just came to say goodbye—and to thank you for your friendship."

It was nearly seven o'clock by this time and the crowd had thinned considerably. Some of those who I presumed to be family members had left, perhaps to have a quick dinner somewhere before returning to the visitation. Junior's widow still stood near the center of the room, talking to a tiny woman who kept nodding her head and patting Mrs. Kandowski on the elbow. I approached the two, but maintained a respectful distance while they finished their conversation. When the tiny woman left, Mrs. Kandowski's smile quickly faded and I could see a weariness and fatigue that couldn't be masked by any amount of determination. "Mrs. Kandowski?" I said as I neared her.

"Yes." The smile returned.

"My name is Will Ross. We've never met, but I knew your husband a long time ago and I wanted to tell you how sorry I am for your loss."

She reached forward and took hold of my hands. "Thank you so much. How did you know Jim?"

"I knew him in high school, and we played football together our sophomore year." She nodded slightly and the smile faded to a faint curvature at the corners of her mouth. "I got to thinking about him when I read he . . . when I saw his obituary. He was such a truly fine young man. I have so many good memories of him. I just felt I needed to honor him somehow."

She squeezed my hands and I saw her eyes glisten with tears. "I'm so glad you came, Mr. Ross. I know Jim would have been delighted that you remembered him." She looked about the room, took a deep breath and straightened up a bit. She continued to hold my hands and gave the appearance she was attempting by sheer force of will to retract the few tears that had gathered in her eyes. "I think you might find some of your old classmates here, if they haven't all left. Those were such important years to Jim. In fact, I think he may have mentioned you when he recalled those days at South, Mr. Ross."

"Please, call me Will."

"Will," she said thoughtfully, appearing to run my name through a lengthy complex of memories. "I'm Helen," she said. "Yes, I'm nearly certain he talked about you and that famous sophomore football team."

We spoke a while longer. I learned that she had met Junior in college—a somewhat comic episode which involved Junior showing up late and in the wrong class on the first day of freshman year. She was struck by his gentleness and kindness and believed, from the moment they first met, that she would spend her life with him. She said she knew that that sounded melodramatic and was very possibly a false memory, but she swore it was absolutely true—and I believed her. As she continued to tell me about their years together, I began to fear that her reminiscing might, at any moment, result in a tearful undoing of her composure, but that didn't happen. She seemed, instead, to draw some sense of comfort and solace from recalling such moments, if only for a stranger.

She recounted how he had loved his work and his family and working as a volunteer at a local community center teaching children to read. She said she knew he wasn't a perfect man, and yet she had no bad memories of him—not one. She seemed surprised as she said it, as if she had never considered that fact until this moment. "There was a reassuring calmness about him, a kind of certainty," she said. She looked beyond me, her eyes unfocused. "It seemed no matter what happened, what disappointments or pain he endured, he saw beyond those little things and understood what was truly important and what truly mattered. And I think we all gained strength from that—the whole family. I know I'm not explaining it well, but he was the kindest, strongest man I ever knew." She looked at me again. "Do you know what I'm trying to say?"

"Yes," I said, "I think I do."

It wasn't long before some of the family members approached and she introduced me to one of her sons, and the chestnut-haired granddaughter who had been periodically assaulting him earlier in the evening. I was also introduced to her daughter, who urged her mother to "please take a break" from the visitation and accompany her while they went to dinner. It seemed an appropriate time for me to say goodbye. Her family was so attentive and clearly so concerned about her that I felt I was keeping her from the respite she so desperately needed. We hugged goodbye and just before she turned to leave with her daughter, she spoke again. "Thank you so much, Will. Jim would have loved that you were here."

When I got outside the funeral chapel, I called Gloria on my cell phone. I told her that I was leaving the visitation but would be delayed just a bit more, as I wanted to take a quick drive through the old neighborhood. She was busy with Mike and obviously distracted but told me not to hurry. She was handling her duties just fine, though Mike was asking why "Papa" wasn't there. "I'll be there within forty-five minutes," I said.

"Okay. How was the visitation? Are you glad you decided to go?"

"I'll tell you about it when I see you. And yes, I'm glad I came here. Kiss Mike for me. I'll see you in just a little while," I told her.

I left the chapel and headed east along the gray city streets to the old neighborhood. It wasn't long before I neared the area where the old high school had stood—now occupied by a housing project. Holy Rosary Church and School remained across the street, and many of the local houses were still recognizable to me. The streets seemed narrower, somehow, and the yards and homes smaller than I remembered, like outgrown clothing of childhood. I drove down several avenues, and then headed west along Twenty-sixth Street to the intersection where Tom had his accident. I crossed through the intersection quickly, being forced by traffic into only a brief glimpse of the corner where he had died. I doubled back to Cedar Avenue and headed south.

The mysterious duality of time and memory struck me as I toured the streets of my youth, how it all seemed so long ago as to belong to another lifetime—even someone else's lifetime—yet at once was no more distant or remote than events of the previous week. How quickly and slowly the years had gone by. And two deaths, separated by more than half a century, filled my thoughts: Tom's, so shocking and violent to any sense of order and logic, and Junior's, so much in harmony with our understanding and expectations of the sweet and tragic design of life. I wondered what might have happened had Tom lived. What might have become of him? Would he have risen above the hostility and anger that surrounded him? Would we still remain friends today? And Junior, what had life truly shown him in his seventy years, what heartbreak and joy? The questions went on and on, so many things unknown and unknowable.

I continued south along Cedar, the streets and sidewalks and houses now bathed in soft, early evening sunlight. I drove beyond Lake Street and Minnehaha Parkway and Lake Nokomis, until at last I reached the freeway. I headed west on the interstate. The sun had now lowered to a point that caused me to shield my eyes with the car's visor. The sunlight glinted and sparkled from the mirrors and windows and bodies of a hundred vehicles streaming in front of me. I sat back deep in my seat and relaxed, letting go of questions about the past and the personalities I'd known. I thought only of the present and my destination, where I would find the gentle affirmations of all that truly matters.